AUBURN TIES

SARAH URQUHART

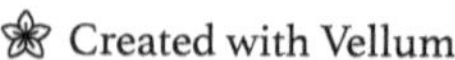 Created with Vellum

Happy Birthday!

ACKNOWLEDGMENTS

I didn't know any details of this story when I first started writing it and if it weren't for trying a new approach to my writing routines, it might never have been written. I have the Level Up Sprint Room to thank for that. And I have to thank everyone in there. You guys are my tribe.

My biggest thanks goes to my beta readers. When I was lost with how the story was structured, you all helped me see the gaps, and more. Thank you, Carrie, Jadzia, Andretta, and Erin.

And thank you to Untold Designs who gave me another beautiful cover. It's perfect.

PROLOGUE

T he door jiggled and Nathan slowly crawled to peek out of his room. He froze, waiting to see who was coming into the house. He held his breath until he saw his mama close the door behind her, but he still didn't move until she turned the lock.

"Nathan, I'm home," her soft voice called, comforting him from a lonely day. He crawled out of his room beneath the stairs. He liked his room, even though it wasn't really a bedroom. A little boy fit perfectly inside the cozy nook. Their house was tiny. The upstairs was a single room filled with boxes. Nathan thought they might be his dad's, but mama wouldn't tell him. His mama slept in the living room.

"Hi, Mama." He wrapped his arms around her legs. She smelled like greasy food and cigarettes, but underneath that he recognized her perfume. She crouched down to the floor to hug him back.

"Did you have a good day today?"

"I did." He nodded solemnly. "I was good too. I stayed in my room the whole time except to go to the bathroom and to get the snacks you left me." There were rules when his mama had to work. He didn't mind, but she said when he got older he would be allowed to do more. She always made him lunch and had snacks ready for him. There weren't many, but if he didn't eat them all at once there was enough for the day. His first day home alone had been scary, but he would be five soon, so he had to be brave like a big kid.

"That's good, Munchkin." She kissed his forehead and went to the kitchen that ran along the back wall opposite his mama's bed.

Nathan rushed to his room to pull out the pictures he drew that day. He'd been practicing drawing animals. "Look, Mama!"

"Wow!" She set the pot down on the burner and turned to face him, excited to see his work. "Is that an elephant?"

"Yeah. Here's his trunk and this is his tiny tail. I'm not sure why such a big animal only has a small tail, but that's what it looked like in my book so that's how I drew it." He moved that picture out of the way to show her the monkey.

"He's so colourful, Nathan. You did a great job."

"Thanks." He puffed his chest out with pride. Nathan ran back to his room to put the pictures up on the wall that was filling up fast. He would have to take some down soon. He pondered which ones were his favourites so he'd know what could go when the time came.

"Dinner's ready." Nathan ran back out while his mama set a bowl on the small table. Excitement jumped inside him when he saw the instant mac-n-cheese.

Not much changed from day to day for Nathan and his mama. When she had a day off work, she always took him to the park or took him out for a picnic. But he spent the rest of his time home alone. His mama said he was still too young for school, but next year he could go because he would be a big kid. He knew he wasn't supposed to be home alone. It's why his mama went over all the rules with him each day. Never answer the door. Never let anyone know he was here. Don't leave his room except to use the bathroom or get snacks. It was important to stay safe.

Nathan had stopped asking what happened to his dad a long time ago. He remembers his face, at least he thinks the face he remembers is his dad. And he remembers the house they used to live in. It was a lot bigger with bigger houses around it that had yards with kids playing in them. But those memories are only frozen images in his mind. This home is all he really knows.

He might not like it, but his mama was always sad, so he needed to be happy for her too. She was working hard to get them a better house. Nathan just had to be patient. They were a team. His mama would always be here for him. She promised him that almost every day.

After dinner, Nathan had his bath then got ready for bed on his own while his mama showered. When she finished, they curled up on her bed while she read him a story and sang him a song. Her voice was soft and no matter how hard he tried, Nathan's eyes always felt heavy when he listened to her sing. She rarely sang the same song two nights in a row. Some nights she sang short songs like *Twinkle Twinkle Little Star* and others she sang longer ones where she stared off in the distance while the tones danced from her lips. Tonight, she sang about seeing him in old places with a park and a carousel.

She lifted him into her arms and carried him to his room. She couldn't fit inside to tuck him in bed, so he put himself in and she crawled in to kiss him goodnight.

"Night, my handsome munchkin."

"Night, Mama. I love you."

"I love you too."

Nathan drifted off to sleep while he listened to his mama clean in the kitchen. It was the same familiar noises every night. She would clean around the house then crawl into her own bed. Sometimes he heard music and others he heard her flipping through pages of a book. But tonight, he fell asleep long before his mama reached her bed.

SOMETHING WOKE NATHAN. He winced and rubbed his eyes. Voices he didn't recognize came from outside his room. And his mama was crying. He tried to listen, but he was too tired to understand. He cracked the tiny door and peeked out.

His mama was on her knees on the floor. So many tears ran down her face, but her eyes widened when she saw him. Even at only four years old, Nathan knew what fear looked like when reflected in his mama's eyes. Wide, shiny, and quivering.

Three strange men stood in the room. Nathan's breathing picked up. One of them stood beside her, pointing something at his mama.

"Where is he?" The voice sent dark vibrations around the room.

"He's dead." Sobs shook her body and her shoulders hunched forward.

"I think you're lying. You thought you could hide from us after he disappeared," said the man behind her, whose black hair was slicked back from his scarred face. "We've been searching for your husband, and you, for two years."

"I don't know anything. But he is dead. I swear it." His mama's voice faded in and out, catching on itself as she spoke.

"I will ask you one last time. Where is your husband?"

said the one pointing the thing at her. Nathan hadn't seen a gun before, but he knew what it was and what it could do. He thought that was a gun.

"Please," she begged. "He's dead. I know nothing about what he did. Please."

The third man that stood against the wall near the kitchen spotted him and walked toward him. Before Nathan could retreat into his room, the man grabbed his arm and pulled him up. Nathan screamed in pain from his grip. Tears pools in his eyes. He didn't want them to escape. He didn't want his mama to see him cry when she was already scared.

"I wonder if she'll tell us if we hurt the kid."

Nathan had to clench his teeth to keep from showing fear.

"No!" his mama screamed. "I swear, if I knew anything I'd tell you. Don't hurt him. I don't have anything to tell you to keep you from hurting him. Please, no."

"She's useless," the scarred-faced guy said in disgust.

So many sensations hit Nathan at once. A deafening bang filled the room. His ears hurt, then started ringing. He watched his mama fall sideways to the floor. Blood spurted from her head and lines of it ran down her face. Nathan went wild, hanging in the air from the third man's grip. His arm twisted painfully, but finally the man dropped him. Ignoring the pain in his knees and arm from the fall, he scrambled up and ran to his mama.

"Please wake up, Mama. You'll be all right. I'm here for you." He looked up at the man with the gun. "Don't hurt her again. Why won't she wake up? Mama?"

"Your mama's dead." The heavy words dropped through the fog in his ears and the man sneered like an ugly dog. He was lying. His mama was right here. Nathan was holding her. Her blood soaked his pajamas, but it would stop soon. She would be all right. She had to be. She'd promised.

Their voices faded beyond the ringing in his ears, but bits and pieces caught his attention. "... the kid?"

"He'll just be a hassle. Might as well..."

The only worry Nathan had had been for his mama, but now he realized he was in danger too. He squeezed his eyes shut and pulled his mama closer as if to protect her from them. So she could protect him.

He heard a click the second before the back door to the house smashed in. The crash forced his eyes open. The frame around the back door was broken, and an enormous hole took the place of where the door used to be.

A giant grizzly bear charged through the tiny house. Sharp teeth and claws tore into the man who shot his mama. Nathan didn't want to watch. He didn't know what would happen to him, but as long as he stayed still, everything would be all right.

He gritted his teeth and held in the tears against the sounds he heard. The bear roaring, the men screaming, and more guns firing. Sounds he didn't know how to explain, but he knew they must be the bear hurting the men, cemented in his memory. He would never forget them. Just like he would never forget this night, this day.

The sounds dragged on, never ending, until suddenly they did. An eerie silence settled around him. Hot breath brushed over the back of Nathan's neck. He shook. He wanted to stay perfectly still, but he couldn't. Something wet and rough ran over his head, moving his hair with it. Nathan slowly loosened his body and turned his head.

The grizzly stood behind him. Big brown eyes and brown fur that looked so fluffy. It didn't growl, but it scared him all the same.

"Please go away, big bear," he whispered. Instead, the bear lay down beside him. Nathan looked around his house for the first time since the bear charged through. He couldn't recognize the men that hurt his mama. There was blood everywhere, and they weren't moving. He looked back down to the only person he had. She was so still. "Mama? Please wake up. You need to be here with me."

Nathan finally allowed the tears to roll down his cheeks. He pulled her close and cried.

By the time the sun rose in the sky, she grew stiff and cold in his arms. He needed to warm her up. He gently set her down and hurried to his room to get all his blankets. The bear lifted its head when he stood, but didn't follow him. Nathan came back and covered up his mama.

"There. You should warm up soon, Mama." He tucked the blankets around her shoulders and waited. A few minutes later, the bear let out a lengthy breath behind him. It stood and nudged Nathan's shoulder. "What do you want?" he asked the bear. The bear gently touched its nose to his mama's chest then nudged Nathan again. Nathan let his hand follow the bear's nose. He laid his hand on her chest. She didn't move or breathe. Did that mean she wasn't ever going to wake up? She could start breathing again. She would wake up.

The bear gently grabbed Nathan's pajama shirt between its teeth and tried to pull him away.

"No!" he screamed. "No! I won't leave her. I need to be here for her to help her get better." The bear let go of him and Nathan hugged his mama. But it was only a moment more and the bear grabbed his shirt again and pulled. Nathan didn't know what was the right thing to do. He gripped tighter. "Goodbye, Mama. I'll come back for you." He whispered the words into her neck and let the bear pull him up and across the room before he got his feet under him. Once he did, he walked beside it.

The sun was bright and low in the sky when they walked out the back door of his house, forcing Nathan to shield his eyes. His stomach churned to be out here in the sun while his mama lay hurt inside. Trees lined the row of tiny houses spaced out on that street. They kept walking until they reached a clearing deeper in the woods.

A baby bear poked its head out from behind a bush and charged at the big one. She was a mama bear. She knocked the baby off her and lay down in the grass. She pulled on Nathan's pajama shirt again until he toppled against her. The baby jumped around him and sniffed. He paused and tilted his head. It was as if he understood something wasn't right with Nathan. He curled up beside Nathan and his mother.

The trees around them moved one by one before a brown twirl of air danced in the space around them. It was pretty, but Nathan didn't care. He wasn't sure what he should do now. But he felt safe cuddling with the bears. The mama bear saved him from the bad men. She was strong enough to protect him.

Nathan watched the wind until his eyes wouldn't stay open any longer. The last thing he remembered was the wind brushing over him and the bear cub, his fur tickling Nathan. It was warm. Nathan didn't realize he had been cold, but he welcomed the feeling. The warmth moved through him while he snuggled further against the bears. He fell into a restless sleep with the horror of his night echoing in his dreams. And awoke hours later as something entirely different than a four-year-old boy.

CHAPTER 1

Nathan rolled his eyes at the name flashing on the screen of his phone vibrating in his hand. He didn't have a problem with the guy, or his intentions, but Nathan couldn't decide if he wanted to be a part of Asher's plans or not.

"Hi, Asher," he said as he put his phone up to his ear, keeping his irritation inside his chest and out of his voice. Nathan got in his truck to head home from work and put the phone on speaker. The lumber mill wasn't a terrible place to work. It was a job, and that's all he cared about. If it didn't work out, he'd find another. But he had been there for almost ten years.

"Hey. Just wondering if you're coming tonight," asked Asher. Nathan heard Gwen, Asher's mate, in the background talking to someone else. The benefits of exceptional shifter hearing.

"Hadn't planned on it." His answer sounded as tired as his weighted body from a day's work.

"I have some news. Nothing urgent, but it's something I'd

like to extend to you." Nathan got the impression there was more than the usual going on.

He sighed. "All right. What time?"

Asher told him and said he'd see him tonight and hung up. He hadn't been the first wolf shifter Nathan discovered, but Asher was the first to talk to him. Nathan never made the initiative to talk to another shifter, or anyone. He didn't care and he didn't want to care. His life was what it was, and Nathan had planned to leave it at that until the wind, his wind, dragged him to Asher's wedding.

At the end of the ceremony, the three winds had danced around a transparent woman off in the distance. White, silver, and auburn swirls had twirled around her like long lost pets who'd found their home. Nathan didn't want to care, but he couldn't stop thinking about the woman's words. The winds were happy and had a purpose to fulfill. It seemed shifters were that purpose.

So, he put up with Asher's phone calls and Gwen's questions, not that he answered many of them. He allowed them to make the connections with him, but didn't put any effort of his own into nurturing those connections. They were good people. He just didn't have a need for people in his life.

And if he were honest, the bond between Asher and Gwen scared the living shit out of him. The strangest scent rushed over him any time he saw Gwen. Everything about her screamed wolf, but she wasn't. She was no longer fully human either. She was some odd mix of magic. Powerful magic that pulled the two of them together in an unbreakable bond.

If that's what it was like for all shifters, he didn't want any part of it. No one deserved to be forced to endure him. And they would be forced. That's what that mating bond did. Asher and Gwen were lucky. They were a good match, but they didn't have a choice. Nathan didn't want that for himself, and he didn't want that for an innocent woman who didn't deserve a strange life. Now he knew that bond existed, he avoided women altogether. Might not be the smartest choice he'd made, but he was sticking to it. For now.

Nathan didn't live in the same shack he had growing up, the one he'd lived in with his mother. Although he'd lived there longer than he should have. Alone. He'd had that roof over his head when he needed it and grew up in the wilderness with no reason to live in town or move to a different one. He'd worked hard and eventually built himself a cabin in the woods. Nathan stayed where he was comfortable.

Bear sauntered out from around the back of the house as Nathan got out of his truck. A four-year-old who'd recently lived through trauma didn't have the best imagination for naming animals. So, he just called him Bear. He never called Bear's mother Mama, despite how she took care of him. He called her Auntie. Nathan had never had one of those.

He shook himself from his thoughts and ran his hand through Bear's fur, feeling the connection of his brother.

"We're meeting at Asher's tonight. Can you get there?" Bear nodded his head then lay down beside the deck. Nathan went inside to shower off the sawdust that covered his skin and left an itch.

He made himself something to eat and threw Bear a fish from his fridge before he left. Sometimes living as a human made his skin crawl, but he knew it was necessary. He had to function in both worlds, and that meant he'd had to catch up to learn as a kid. And he did that on his own. Once he finally shifted back to human, a child. No one had ever found him after his mother disappeared. They thought she disappeared. Nathan knew the truth. But they had also been looking for a little boy.

Pulling up behind Asher's truck, Nathan saw the motorcycle parked beside it. Zachary, another wolf shifter, was also here. He couldn't figure out Zachary's reasons for meeting with Asher anymore than he could figure out his own. Nathan didn't think he held onto a similar vision as Asher's future for shifters. A society for their own species. The only reason of which Nathan was certain was Zachary's need to be close to his pair. Pair being the term Asher used for their matched animals. Nathan didn't bother calling his anything but his bear. Maybe brother on occasion.

Zachary and his wolf had been separated for a couple years. That was all Nathan knew and all he cared to know.

He walked toward the trees and met up with Bear not far in before hiking to their usual meeting spot. He smelled the four wolves and Gwen, pinpointing their positions long before they reached them.

"Hi, Nathan," Gwen's cheerful tone rose as he got closer. She was a sweet girl who tried her best to be worthy of her mate. She took on the role as mate to a wolf shifter with pride and determination. Yeah, Asher got lucky.

Nathan waved back but kept quiet. He rarely said much at these *meetings.* Asher called them meetings, but once they had all told their stories and the things they'd learned over the years, there was nothing else to discuss. They only gathered to shoot the shit. Although Nathan still hadn't told them about his past. He wasn't sure if he ever would. It was none of their damn business.

"Glad you could make it." Asher stood beside his wife, his mate. It became natural for them to interchange the two. Even Nathan referred to her as a mate, despite her not being his. Asher had a point when he referred to them as a different species. They had instincts they didn't realize existed. Callings and whispers from within.

Nathan nodded, then nodded at Zachary who stood off to the side.

"I'm building a cabin," Asher announced and nodded toward the white wolf standing near. "Deeper in the woods. Close to Kai's pack, although the space and terrain around the area has many places for wildlife. I want it to be a safe house, or a headquarters, for us and other shifters we meet. A place that will always be stocked with nonperishables and clothes. I want you both to feel welcome to use it."

"When will it be finished?" asked Zachary.

"A few months, most likely more. It'll take a little longer as we can't use big equipment to build it. I won't destroy the forest to build a haven inside it."

"Need help?"

"Probably." Asher nodded. They all looked at Nathan. Well, hell. He didn't want to be dragged further into their shifter club, but here he stood anyway.

"Yeah, let me know if there's anything I can do," he said, the words pulling themselves out of his throat.

"You work at a lumber yard." Zachary pointed out.

"I work there. I don't own it. I can't do more than tell you the cost and who to talk to about the purchase."

"Thank you," said Asher, as if that's all he was looking for.

"A place like that could be useful." Zachary agreed with the idea from a distance. Nathan noticed Zachary's wolf near him, stiff with tension still holding pain coiled inside. Each of the shifters felt it. Whatever happened between the two of them still needed resolving. No one knew why Zachary had abandoned his wolf. Smoke stayed with Kai and his pack, and Zachary was trying to reconnect with Smoke.

Nathan couldn't imagine any scenario that would keep him from Bear. But he grew up differently than either of the wolves.

"I need to call it a night. See you next time."

"You sure you have to go so soon?" It surprised Nathan to hear Zachary ask. It was usually Asher that tried to encourage Nathan to stay.

"Yeah." He waved and nodded to Bear before heading back to his truck. The others enjoyed these meetings, making plans for the future with an independence they thought they'd never have. That was great for them, but Nathan still didn't want to be part of it more than he already was. And if it hadn't been for that damn wind and the woman at the wedding, he wouldn't be.

Shaye threw the last bag in the back of her truck. Now, she waited for Jerry, Jenna, and Chase. The only friends that had been by her side since they were teenagers and the only friends she made time for. She pulled down the tailgate and used her palms to jump up. This was their first camping trip of the year. Excitement hummed through Shaye. As the assistant to the top realtor in Alder Ridge, she had to always be ready to move at the drop of a hat and never have a detail out of place, always busy.

She craved the peace of the lake. She kept one of her old cell phones to use for camping. No smartphones allowed for her, and while camping it was only for emergencies. She wouldn't be stupid and go into the wilderness without some form of contact. But she safely tucked away her smartphone in her nightstand. Taking away all temptation and contact with work. Camping was the most vacation she got between work and her friends, and she was fine with that. As far as she was concerned, there wasn't anything better.

But relaxing didn't describe her life. It was the office life for her. Except the times like these when she chose otherwise.

Shaye's lips lifted with anticipation to breathe in the air off the lake. They didn't travel far for their camping trips. They didn't need to. Alder Ridge had beautiful landscapes and wilderness surrounding it and beyond. Thanks to the town's proximity to the mountains.

Her love of camping and all things wild came from her dad. He had done great at the single parent thing. They'd bonded as best friends. Shaye's fingers turned over the locket around her neck and she allowed only a moment of sadness. She sent up a quick prayer, then started swinging her legs in the air while she watched the road for her friends. Some things didn't need to be thought about at a time like this. No matter how much she missed her father, she wouldn't let it sadden her camping trip. Not when it had been the most shared activity between them.

Finally, a blue Jeep pulled up and her three friends barrelled out with whoops and hollers. Shaye hopped off the tailgate and closed it.

"Throw your bags in the back. I'm ready to go."

"Always in such a rush, Shaye." Jerry nudged her shoulder as he passed carrying two bags.

"Until she gets in the woods, then she's all mellow," said Jenna, extending the last of her words and swaying her shoulders side to side. Shaye shrugged off the teasing of her friends.

Chase touched Shaye's elbow before she could climb into the driver's seat. "Why don't you let me drive?"

Shaye reared back and raised an unbelieving brow. "You are not driving my truck." The rest of the group laughed, and she threw a smug expression at her friend's envy. His old beater had finally given out last week. Shaye swung back around and hopped in with a bounce. She'd worked hard for this truck. It was her baby. She wouldn't let just anyone drive it, no matter how close a friend they were.

She started the truck and waited for everyone to pile in. Chase sat in the front and Jenna and Jerry sat in the back, Jerry's arm pulling her tight against him.

"And we're off." Shaye cranked the radio and sped off.

The drive out to the lake only took half an hour. It wasn't a regular campground, but it wasn't uncommon for locals to rough it by the lake. Shaye preferred to rough it. It didn't feel like camping to her if there were amenities, roads, trails, and playgrounds. Her friends didn't like it much, preferring to find a glorified space with the brick fire pit, firewood already stacked, and full showers. But they knew she wouldn't camp with them if they went anywhere else.

She set up her small one-person tent, then helped her struggling friends with their larger one. Chase sidled up to Shaye when they finished.

"Please don't make me share a tent with Jerry and Jenna. They're insufferable." He lowered his head and his voice. Shaye shrugged.

"I told you to bring your own tent. Mine isn't big enough." Shaye walked off to finish setting up, enjoying the pout on the man's face. She should be sympathetic, but she didn't like to share her dad's tent.

She organized the coolers and settled them in the truck's cab so the food wouldn't attract bears and other wildlife.

Once finished, she set up a fire pit and built the fire. That's all she cared about. Sitting by a fire, fishing, and swimming in the lake, an escape and reset for her mind and body. She might live and work in town, but this was where she belonged.

"How do you always make this look so easy?" Jenna unfolded her chair and plopped down beside Shaye, having finished setting up their tent and throwing their bags inside.

"Because it is easy." Shaye passed her a beer.

"Jenna, she's been doing this since she was two. It's not easy. She just knows what the fuck she's doing." Jerry looked at Jenna as if she asked a stupid question. Their camping trips always started with this same conversation. Shaye let it roll over her every time. Once they got it out of their systems, they all moved on and everyone had a great time.

Shaye let the wilderness settle in while they finished their banter. Once the conversation lulled, she stood. "I'm going fishing."

She saw Chase pull a ten-dollar bill from his pocket and hand it over to Jerry.

"Told you, man," said Jerry.

"Told him what?" Shaye's eyes darted between the two guys.

"That you would go fishing as soon as we all sat down." Jerry lifted his hip and tucked the bill in his back pocket.

"I don't do that every time." She looked at each of her friends.

"Yes, you do," they all said in unison.

"We know you do it so you can be alone. It's okay, Shaye." Jenna reached out and touched her hand. Sympathy echoed in her quiet voice.

Shaye huffed and walked to her truck to get her gear. Did she do this every time just so she could be alone? She didn't do it intentionally. But she also wouldn't deny she enjoyed the quiet by the water. Her friends would come fish with her once or twice on their trip, but Shaye knew that was only to spend time with her. They'd rather swim, then get drunk by the fire.

Shaye let it go. These trips were for clearing her head, not dwelling on her habits. She cherished this time away. Nothing would ruin it.

Nathan couldn't sleep. He woke in the night, tangled in sheets and drenched with sweat. So many sounds and smells haunted his dreams. Campfire smoke, laughter, singing, his mama's voice, the creek of a swing set, men's voices, the scent of death and gunpowder. He cursed and opened his eyes to stare up at the ceiling, but saw a translucent brown swirl.

"Fuck off." He groaned and tried to straighten his blankets and go back to sleep, but the wind pushed his bedding down and ruffled his hair. "Fuck off," he repeated. When the wind wouldn't let him pull his blankets back, he sighed and got out of bed. The wind followed him to the kitchen.

He pulled the milk from the fridge and tipped the jug back, taking a healthy chug. The wind moved, fluttering with impatience, beside him. Nathan put the milk away and slammed the fridge door. He stomped to the front of his house, threw open the door and stepped onto the porch.

"Bear!" he yelled. After a moment, Bear sauntered out from the side, sleep pulling each limb downward with a thump as he walked. "Anything wrong?" The animal shook his head. "Any idea what this wants?" Nathan pointed with his thumb to the wind beside him and again Bear shook his head. "Good." Bear sagged as he left and Nathan spun on his heel and went inside, slamming his door.

The wind swirled around him, stopping him on his way back to bed.

"I said fuck off!" roared Nathan. The wind froze and drooped in the air, a brown waterfall frozen in place. "I'm not interested, so if it isn't an emergency, leave me the fuck alone." Nathan wouldn't ignore it if it was, but he knew what the wind acted like for an emergency, and this wasn't it. Still, he threw the question out there, just in case.

The wind drifted away, sulking like a scolded child. Nathan sighed, regret eating his insides.

No. He didn't care. Nathan wasn't interested in anything shifter unless he had to be. He wasn't an asshole. He just didn't want anything dragging him into another world other than his own.

Nathan fell back into bed, but didn't sleep. Terror of what awaited him behind closed eyes kept him awake. The images in his dreams didn't match each other. More than one dream had been happening at once. And the scents were vivid, as if he were there, wherever there was.

After an hour of useless effort, he rose, taking his rarely used computer from the nightstand to the kitchen table. He opened the file from Asher containing the plans for the cabin. He did the math to figure out the amount of lumber he would need and the cost, made a few tweaks to the design, and sent it back to Asher. Nathan couldn't deny the idea was a good one. A safe house for any shifter that comes along. Even if his plans were a little premature, they were good.

There may only be three of them at this point, but they

would grow. They wanted a safe place away from homes and away from eyes. Nathan wasn't lining up to get caught, so he wouldn't argue. He'd even decided it was in his best interest to help.

By the time the sun rose, Nathan had his fourth cup of coffee and was ready for work. When he stepped outside, the wind still hovered in a tree across from his house. His eyes flashed and his ears pricked. Something was out there. Something changed in his woods. He shook his head and looked at Bear.

"You don't sense it do you?" The enormous animal shook his head and roamed off. Some help he was. Nathan jogged to his truck and drove off, reminding himself he didn't care.

Once at the lumber yard, he put in the order for Asher and labeled it with his name and contact information. They would call Asher when they had it ready.

Nathan worked until lunch, his job full of mindless tasks. Most of the men knew not to bother talking to him, and those that didn't soon figured it out. But whatever invaded his dreams and his space the night before, hovered over him now. Then when he saw a brown swirl near the gate, he just about lost his patience. His eyes on the gate, he intended to charge across the yard, but Asher stepped in front of him. Nathan reared back and glared at the man brave enough to step in front of someone that had a grizzly bear soul.

"You okay?"

"Sure."

"What does it want?" Asher nodded behind him toward the wind.

"Don't know, don't care." He sighed. "You here to get your order?"

"Yeah. That was fast. I appreciate you putting it through for me."

"Yeah. No problem."

Asher stared at him for a moment. "Do you think it's smart to ignore it?"

"Probably not, but like I said, I don't care."

Asher lifted his hands and walked away. "Okay. But if it's something you need help with, you know you can call."

Nathan nodded. He knew it, but he didn't have to like it. He wasn't about to thank Asher for it either. Nathan gave one last look at the wind, then turned to go back to work.

THE NEXT AFTERNOON, Shaye spent her fishing excursion helping Jenna. Between knots in the line, a stuck reel, the *gooey* bait, and the actual fish, Shaye didn't have time to set up her own before the rest of the gang declared enough and it was time for dinner and drinking.

Shaye inwardly sighed. She wouldn't show them her disappointment. Gathering her gear, she followed them back to the campsite, cheering the guys' catches. She didn't put it away, knowing she would try to sneak out first thing in the morning. They all slept late, except for her. At home, she was never a morning person. But out here was different in every way, and that included her sleeping habits.

Since she caught nothing, she didn't have any fish to clean. She and Jenna got to tend the fire with beer already in their hands while the guys prepped the fish to cook. So, she supposed she couldn't complain too much. Her and Jenna got to start their own fun before the guys.

Shaye often wondered if she would ever trade her job or her life in town for one like this. It crossed her mind with every camping trip. But she never could come up with a good reason not to. She twisted her lips with the fanciful thought. Despite having so little free time, she enjoyed her job. It didn't matter that she longed to be here whenever she wasn't.

Last year, she tried to come out toward the end of fall, winter had hung in the air, but Jenna stopped her by waylaying her with fake issues. For whatever reason, her friends thought she should never go camping alone. She didn't understand what they were so afraid of, but Shaye had appeased them and waited. She made them camp often during the summer, even dragging them out here for the holidays and well into fall. But as soon as the first frost hit, they all refused to budge. Sadly, this far north, the first frost sometimes hit late September, then hit again through October. It wasn't that they didn't enjoy camping, but Shaye's style of camping wasn't their favourite.

"If you girls are just going to sit there, why don't you at least put some music on," called Jerry. Shaye and Jenna stuck out their tongues at his retreating back. They giggled like they used to in middle school when talking about the boys and writing their names in their notebooks.

Jenna pulled out her phone while she grabbed her speaker from her tent. She put on her latest playlist creation and sat back down. "If they want music, they'll have to deal with my choices." Jenna clinked her bottle against Shaye's. Shaye joined in her conspiratorial grin and drank.

She and Jenna had been friends since grade five. If it weren't for Jenna, Shaye might never have been able to pull herself out of that dismal, dark hole she leapt into after graduation, after her father's accident. No matter what kind of peace Shaye looked for, she would never push Jenna away. She was the sister she never had or knew she needed.

As the night wore on and the campfire stories and drunken singing had ended, Chase and Shaye watched as Jenna's and Jerry's hands gave themselves more freedom. The alcohol doing what it did for most couples. It would be a noisy night in their tent. Chase grabbed his chair and moved it beside Shaye. She slowly shook her head.

"You are not sleeping in my tent."

"Seriously? You're really going to make me sleep next to them doing that."

"Yup. I told you to bring your own tent, and I even told you why. Doesn't matter what your sensitive eyes will be witness to, you're not sleeping with me." Shaye took a pull of her beer and tossed a fake sweet smile at Chase.

"You're mean," he said with no heat.

"And you're a dumbass for not bringing your own tent." She raised her brows, holding in her laughter.

He sighed and left to get another beer, his eyes glaring at her as he walked away. His lips pinched, turning his mock displeasure up a notch before his face relaxed.

The fire dimmed and Shaye had had enough company for one day. "Night, everyone." She waved to no one in particular, knowing they weren't paying any attention to her anyway, and went to bed. She looked forward to her early morning alone at the lake.

NATHAN CURSED as sweat and dreams woke him again. And again, the wind hovered above him.

"What the fuck do you want? Are you the one doing this to me? Are you invading my dreams and turning them into painful nonsense?" The wind didn't answer him. Never did. Never would. It led him where he needed to go. Whatever the wind's purpose, that was part of it. But it wasn't trying to take him anywhere, now.

He stood from the bed and almost fell backward as his senses fired in an instant, forcing his head to swirl. It was the same sense he had that morning when he left for work caused by a disturbance in his woods. A frustrated huff escaped his lungs. The campfire he smelled in his dreams. He smelled it now. Fucking campers. They must be too close to his territory.

Nathan stretched and went to get a drink, feeling dehydrated. When he got back to his bed, the wind was still there. He didn't have the energy to yell again.

"Just go away." He fell back into his bed as his stomach curled and his head pounded. What the fuck was wrong with him? Shifters didn't experience normal sickness. An upset stomach and headache were new.

He tossed and turned in bed for hours, trying to calm his senses, calm his nerves. His bedroom spun in circles around him. Standing felt impossible, but he couldn't lay here any longer. Sleep wouldn't happen. He needed out. Part of him knew he didn't want to shift. It might be what he needed to do, but it wasn't what he wanted.

He stood, then fell to his knees with a thud. He heard the first pops of his body changing. "No," he growled. His body tensed and he forced the shift to stop. He could control this. He would control this.

Nathan crawled back into his bed, agony overtaking him. He slipped in and out of consciousness, his wakeful dreams haunting and painful. He'd thrown his pillow across the room hours ago and his sheets were twisted into a knot beside him.

Urges and senses called to him. He didn't want to shift, and he didn't want to endure this torment. He wasn't territorial. But this time, whatever was in his woods bothered him. Pulled him to do things he didn't understand.

His eyes flew open, but they weren't his. His bear's eyes heated and his vision changed. Damn it. He had to get out of the house before he finished shifting. He didn't trust himself not to smash his door or the rest of his house as a bear with his current state. As a shifter, he was larger than normal. He built his own house. In hindsight, he should have made his space and doors bigger.

Nathan staggered, catching himself on the wall before he fell to the floor. He groaned while he pulled himself back up and somehow made his way to his front door. Bear already waited for him outside, knowing something wasn't right with Nathan.

With hands and knees sinking into the ground, his body shifted. Shifting was never painful, but right now, Nathan roared into the night as parts moved out of place with painful screams. His muscles and joints were taught and stiff with the effort to fight off the change. Soon, the pain of fighting it was too much and Nathan let go.

By the time fur covered his body and his claws dug into the earth beneath him, he was panting and heaving for breath. Bear stood in front of him.

Are you okay? He asked with fear pushing through his thoughts.

I don't know. Something is drawing me away. I need to move. Trespassers never bothered him before, so he didn't understand why it bothered him now. But as a bear, his senses sharpened and he had more control. The animal instincts were all he could hear. He ran away, following those instincts.

The disturbance, the campers, were further away than he'd imagined. This wasn't a place he considered his territory. He crept around their campsite. One scent that rose above all, citrus and pine.

His nose twitched while he searched around the campfire, then around the big tent. Three people inside. It reeked of cologne and sex. Nathan cringed and circled. Around the other side sat a black truck. The truck belonged to that scent. Their food was stored inside, and the back held a couple bags and fishing gear.

Nathan looked to his left and did a double take. A small tent big enough for an individual sat off to the side, a little further from the fire pit than the other. He stalked over, his nose going wild. There. Citrus and pine rose from within. Lifting his paw, he clawed at the zipper until it lifted an inch, enough for him to see the tent was empty. Nose to the ground, he followed the scent.

His mind screamed to go back home, ignore what was happening. But as a bear, he wouldn't allow himself. It was why he couldn't control his shift. His animal half and the wind wouldn't let him ignore Fate. The bitch.

The sun sat just above the horizon and the dawn was dim with the trees blocking the light until he got closer to the lake. Blonde hair shone and citrus assaulted his nose. An auburn swirl moved her hair and rushed her scent at Nathan. The fucking wind. He found his mate.

All four of his legs weakened and he fell to the ground as her scent penetrated his body. He fought with his own thoughts and it exhausted him. Soon, his animal instincts told himself to shut up, and that's all he was. A bear looking at his mate, eager to claim her as his.

CHAPTER 3

Shaye had been silent leaving her tent, although she hadn't needed to be. The other three had been up well into the night and would sleep until at least noon. There wasn't much that would wake them before the sun was even up.

She'd grabbed her gear from the back of the truck, happy she hadn't packed it all away the day before. Joy had filled her as she walked down to the lake. She only had another day, maybe two here. Convincing her friends to stay a full week never worked out for her, but most of the time she got them to stay an extra day. They would expect it. And they would never let her stay the full week without them. Hence the reason they all piled into her truck for every trip. She didn't understand why they believed she should never be left alone. This was the first trip she'd ever given the behaviour much thought.

She could stop telling them what she was doing, but that wouldn't be right. As her best friends, she told them everything.

Shaye held her breath when her line went taut and she

pulled back. The weight on the end of the line while reeling it in, told her it wasn't big. She'd caught several so far, but nothing she could keep. She was okay with that. A meal wasn't the purpose this morning.

So lost in her task, she didn't notice the bear approaching until it was a few feet away from her along the bank. Shaye swallowed her scream, the small fish, gasping for life in her hand, poised to throw back. The bear stood panting, his breath moving his lips outward from his jaw. His nose, wet and black, twitched. With slow movements, she stood. She'd intended to release the fish, but it was either the bear's favourite slimy treat or her. She chose the fish. *Sorry, little guy.*

Shaye tossed the fish in front of the bear. "Take it. Now move." She gathered all her courage to make her tiny self seem bigger than the bear, ready to yell and roar with all her might at the first sign of aggression from the bear.

He sniffed the fish, then swatted it, sending it flying back into the water. *Well, you're free, little guy. Guess it's me then.* The bear didn't make a sound. He didn't charge, but he moved closer with slow steps. Shaye's body shook with fear, but she took a deep breath to control it. She had to, her life depended on it. Of all people on this camping trip, she was the one stupid enough to leave her bear spray back at the camp. Out of sight, out of running distance. Camp was a few minute hike away. The only things near were a few trees and the lake right beside her.

He pressed his nose to her chest and inhaled. She stood with her arms ready at her sides and her feet in a sturdy stance spread apart. But her insides froze, like millions of tiny cubes floating through her body. Her skin tightened and a cold sweat dampened her back.

The bear smelled her neck. If he turned aggressive right

then, she wouldn't have time to make herself seem bigger and fiercer, not with him nuzzling her most vulnerable body part.

The bear walked around her. She squeezed her eyes shut while the animal was behind her for fear he would choose the moment she couldn't see it coming to attack. She felt his nose at her hip, and he moved inward. Her eyes flew open as he inhaled between her legs. What the hell was this bear doing?

He stepped back and shook his head as if shaking something stuck in his fur. His brown eyes bore into hers. They were bright and rich with so much power behind them. Shaye's breath was shallow with the effort to stay still and not react. He backed up a few more steps, then lay down.

Chancing that it was safe to move, she took a step sideways up the bank, but didn't turn away from the bear. She took a second step and the bear opened his enormous mouth, a short growl escaping. He lifted a front paw and stomped it on the ground in front of him. Shaye froze and waited for him to calm.

She counted to sixty in her head and tried again. Two steps sideways up the bank. The bear's jaw opened and moved in a circle with the sound of his growl. He slapped his paw again, then nodded toward the lake.

"What is it?" she asked, using a soft voice she'd use on a child. "You don't want me to leave?" He only stared at her until she tried to take another step up the bank. This time his growl was sharper, and he braced himself to stand. "Okay, okay. I'll stay."

She had to be crazy. She was staying with a grizzly bear of her own free will. Because he demanded it. She mentally shook her head and moved back to her fishing rod. She kept her eyes locked with the bear's while she bent and picked it up. He laid his head down on the ground in front of him. Fishing would give her something to do and by his relaxed position, he didn't care as long as she didn't leave.

Shaye wasn't able to keep her body from shaking any longer. Her anxious nerves and fear let loose now that her muscles relaxed from the danger she'd been in, was still in. Sitting down on the bank, she pulled in several deep breaths. She didn't believe the danger was gone. There was still a grizzly a few feet away from her who wanted her to sit with him and fish. Now, this was a camping story.

While watching him from the corner of her eye, eyes that were filling with unshed tears of fear, Shaye readied another lure and bait, with trembling hands. She cast her line. Unsettled was an understatement for how she felt. Terror zipped through her system with such a large wild predator watching her. She couldn't turn aggressive to scare him away, not that that would work with this bear anyway, and she couldn't go back to camp.

Shaye pulled in three fish, two to keep, one to throw back. The bear's head lifted and his attention turned toward camp. He stood and Shaye tensed. Brown eyes pinned her in place so she didn't dare stand up. His foot stomped the ground before he backed away into the bushes, his flashing eyes barely visible.

"I hate to ask how long you've been up." Jenna slogged her way toward Shaye with a yawn. Shaye slowly spun around, but didn't stand. This could be her chance to escape back to camp, but she didn't dare. Anything that would anger the bear hiding in the bushes would put Jenna in danger.

"Yeah, you probably wouldn't like the answer." Shaye cringed when her voice cracked. Jenna paused. Her already sleepy narrowed eyes twitched as if to scowl at her, but they didn't have enough room for the reaction.

"Shaye, are you all right? You're so pale."

"Yeah, I'm fine. I must still be tired."

"I wouldn't fault you for going back to bed. Any normal person would." Jenna started to sit down beside her.

"Why don't you take these back up to camp?" Shaye passed her bucket to Jenna before she hit the ground. She needed to at least keep Jenna safe. "Stick them in the cooler for me. We can have them later."

"Shaye, we can't eat fish for the entire trip." Her shoulders sagged.

"I don't care what we eat. But you're still tired. You don't need to keep me company down here. Go hang out by the fire and make some coffee."

"You sure, Shaye?"

"Of course. I shouldn't be much longer." They heard a low grunt and foot hitting the ground. Jenna spun around, her tired eyes widening with sudden alertness, searching the bushes.

"What was that?" They both stared at the bush. Shaye searched for the brown eyes, but she couldn't find them. Everything was still and quiet. The words were a whisper tickling the tip of her tongue. *It's a bear. I need you to calmly walk back to camp and get one of the guys to bring down the bear spray.*

"There's nothing there. Go on back. I'll see you in a bit." Different words escaped.

Jenna took the bucket and walked back to camp. Shaye looked back at the bushes and saw the brown eyes flash again and the bear poked his head out.

"So, you expect me to stay down here all day?" No answer, no gesture, no sign of understanding. "I can't, you know. My friends will keep coming to check on me and then eventually they'll either drag me back to camp or move the camp down here." The bear only huffed, not caring about her problems.

Shaye caught one more fish, again too small to keep, but so close. The sun further above the horizon meant at least an hour had passed since Jenna came searching for her. She heard footsteps approaching the same time the bear ducked back into the bush.

"Shaye?" Chase sat down beside her. "Are you all right? Jenna's worried about you."

"I'm fine. Just taking my time down here. Like I always do, remember?" She didn't realize she held a touch of bitterness over the guys' bet the day before.

"Why don't you come back up with me? Hang out for a while. We're thinking of packing up soon."

"I'll drive you guys back, but I'm staying another night."

"To do what? We want to hang out with you too."

She gave him a flat expression and shook her head.

"Damn it. I owe Jerry another ten dollars." He hit his forehead on his knees. Shaye didn't like being a game to them.

"You really thought you could convince me to go home, didn't you? Enough that you bet on it?"

"Yup." He sighed. "Don't stay down here much longer. Jenna isn't the only one that's worried."

"I'm not sure why you're all so worried about me." Shaye shook her head.

"You seriously don't know why?"

"No. There's no reason to be." Shaye searched his face, hoping to find an answer.

Chase scoffed and shook his head. He looked as if he had a reason to be upset with her. He stood and walked away, his body sagging. A streak of self-doubt niggled at Shaye as she watched his retreating back. She didn't understand, and none of her friends offered an explanation.

She looked back at the bushes as the bear walked out of them. Guess there was something for them to worry about this time. A demanding grizzly bear that wouldn't allow her to leave.

NATHAN COULDN'T KEEP her here by the lake. Oh, he wanted to. He didn't want to let her out of his sight, but her friends weren't going to either.

Listening to her friend's footsteps fade away, Nathan walked over to her. She stood and her body tensed, ready to defend herself. He had no control over his actions. He nuzzled his nose into her chest as if he didn't already have enough of her scent ingrained in his core. Nathan stayed there until she relaxed. Her hand lifted.

That's it sweetness. Touch me. His skin tightened, craving a touch he hadn't known he needed. Her tiny fingers laced through his fur on his neck. Tremors ran through her stomach and her fingers shook on his skin.

"You're softer than I imagined a bear would be. And you guys look damn soft." Her voice was choppy and her body too stiff for his liking. He nuzzled her again and moved his nose down to her stomach. "You're awfully friendly for a bear. And demanding," she added as an afterthought. "Am I allowed to go back to camp now?"

Nathan huffed. He nudged her hip toward her camp then stomped his paw and nodded at the lake. He'd let her go, but he intended she come back because he wasn't going anywhere.

"I can leave, but you want me to come back?" she asked. He repeated his movements, nudging her up the bank then stomping the ground. "Okay. I'll come back later."

Nathan closed his eyes and inhaled before walking back to the bush where he would wait for her. If she didn't come back on her own, he would go find her. He didn't care who would see him. She couldn't hide from him.

Shaye gathered her gear, the longest moment she took her eyes off him. She looked to the bushes and he let her see his eyes. His body tensed, ready to chase after her, as he watched her walk away. He growled low in his chest, freeing his frustrations. He never wanted to find his mate, but the words echoed in his head and after listening to Asher describe his experience, he knew what she was. Maybe he could have walked away if he had controlled his shift, but as a bear, only animal instincts reigned.

Fighting the call turned out to be some of the most intense agony he'd ever experienced. If he tried to pull away from her now and continue to fight the bond... he worried about the consequences. Nathan had some decisions to make. First being how he would handle this. She knew a bear, not a man. If his animal continued to rule, he would drag her back to his cabin and keep her there, but that wasn't a great way to start a relationship.

Nathan grunted. What did he know about relationships? It might be easier to be blunt and tell her what he is and who she is to him. Easier for him. Fuck, this would be painful no matter how he handled it. Could he come back as a man and manipulate her, not telling her who he was? He wasn't an actor. For now, she expected a bear. A bear is what she'd find.

He listened to them at the camp. Her friends wanted to leave, but his mate didn't. It didn't seem to come as a surprise to her friends, but they argued with her all the same. They refused to leave her and she refused to leave. Until tomorrow. He had until then to act, or he would have to turn Alder Ridge upside down looking for her. Assuming she lived in Alder Ridge. He had a scent and her name to go on.

Shaye. She was small and fit, blonde and beautiful, and loved being out here, capable of looking after herself. Although her friends disagreed. He could sense her happiness and content before she saw him. Sitting on the bank by the water, she wasn't troubled. He recognized her contentment, her sense of belonging.

Nathan grew impatient by the time she returned to the lake, but she wasn't alone. All three of her friends followed her down. His lips curled, ready to growl and scare them all away, but stopped, barely. They all took their clothes off, the girls revealing swimsuits, the guys already wearing shorts. His eyes focused on Shaye.

Fit, tan, the perfect curves. Fuck, she was gorgeous. And not wearing near enough fabric to cover her. He groaned.

Her friends started wading in the water, but she stayed back and looked over at the bushes. Nathan let his eyes flash, and he heard her sharp intake of breath when she saw them. *Yes, sweetness. I'm still here.*

"Shaye!" She tore her eyes away from him and followed her friends into the water. Part of him was evil enough to consider jumping into the water with them all. But the last thing he wanted was her friends banning Shaye from leaving camp on her own because of a bear.

Nathan braced himself for torture while he watched her swim.

"HEY, SHAYE. YOU COMING?" Jenna called back when Shaye paused on the bank after their swim.

"Yeah, in a bit. I'm going to dry out down here."

"Well, I need the fire. That water was cold!" Jenna followed the boys back to camp. Shaye was thankful for the chilly water. She couldn't explain feeling so overwhelmed when she saw the bear's eyes. The cool temperature had drawn her back to reality.

She laid her towel down on the grass and sat, leaning back on her hands. She waited. The bear's presence was a physical thing. He would come out now that she was alone. This was the strangest experience she'd ever had with any animal, let alone a wild animal. A smart animal, she thought.

He emerged from the bushes and stalked toward her. His eyes narrowed and pinned her in place. A sliver of fear resurfaced. There was no reason for her to believe he wouldn't hurt her. Their exchange earlier was friendly, but unusual behaviour. She took deep, steadying breaths into her quaking body. He tilted his head, but didn't stop or slow his progress.

With her sitting on the ground, he towered over her. What was she thinking making herself easy prey? He looked down at her and she tilted back. His nose ruffled her hair before he lay down beside her, resting his head on his paws.

"I told you I'd come back. Now, what?" The bear lifted his head and pushed it forward, so it rested on her legs instead. She forgot to breathe for a moment, then her hand moved of its own accord. She ran it over his head and watched him close his eyes. "No one would ever believe this."

He huffed. Now that he had her pinned to the ground she wondered if he would let her go at all this time.

"You know I can't stay. Not today. And I'll be going home

tomorrow." He huffed again. "You're going to let me go, aren't you?" He lifted his head only an inch then set it heavily on her lap again. Guess that answered her question. He seemed to understand her, so maybe she could bargain with him.

"Tell you what, you let me leave to go back to camp and leave tomorrow to go home, and I'll come back alone. Deal?" His eyes opened and rolled upward. He didn't deny her in any way she could understand. But he moved his head to nuzzle against her stomach, his nose reaching to run over her breasts. He was a seriously friendly animal.

A moment later, he lifted his head off her and let out a low rumble toward their camp. He took one last poke at her neck and jogged back to the bushes, his fur shaking over his curves and limbs.

"You shouldn't stay down here alone for so long." They'd sent Jerry to fetch her this time.

"What's wrong with being down here alone?"

"Come on, Shaye. You know we all worry about you. Don't isolate yourself." He sighed and rolled his eyes.

"I do know that you all worry, but I don't know why."

"You aren't stupid, Shaye," he snapped. The word stupid carried harsh edges that hit the surrounding air. He shook his head. "Come on. Let's go." He didn't cajole her, he demanded. It pissed Shaye off, being treated like she was a walking threat to herself. Especially when she didn't know where it came from. It had been this way for years, but never before had their protectiveness turned so fierce. "Let's go, Shaye. Get up." Jerry snapped again and took a step toward her.

A growl echoed from the bushes and Jerry whirled around. Shaye couldn't stop the smirk on her lips. Thankfully, Jerry wasn't looking at her. "What is it?"

"Did you hear that?" His words ran together and his tone dropped to a whisper.

"No. You're jumpy, Jerry." She stood on her own and put her clothes on over her now dry swimsuit and picked up her towel. Jerry still stood frozen, staring at the bushes. "You coming?" Shaye walked off, not waiting for him to catch up, and hoped the bear was willing to stick to their deal.

She would need to have a talk with her friends soon. The way they had been treating her lately was unacceptable. They were the only people in her life. She'd always trusted them, but she wouldn't blindly follow demands that stemmed from concern when they wouldn't talk to her.

CHAPTER 4

Nathan stretched and rolled his neck as twilight blanketed the sky and the moon shone on the water. Once Shaye and her friends settled in at their camp, Nathan emerged from hiding and waded into the lake, getting a drink and snagging a fish to eat. He slept on the bank and allowed the night air to dry his fur. Now, he watched and listened, hoping Shaye would return to see him.

She didn't disappoint him.

Light footsteps made their way through the trees. Nathan waited.

"This is the last time I can come see you. We're leaving first thing in the morning. Do we still have a deal?" She raised her brow, waiting for an answer that wouldn't come.

It didn't matter what their deal was. If she didn't come back, he would find her.

"My friends would have a fit right now if they found out I came back down here." She sat down on the grass beside him. "Not because of you, but they'd have a fit over that too. I wish I knew what they worried about. Maybe I should worry about myself. I'm meeting up with a grizzly and having a conversation with him." A half smile lifted her lips. "I'd be lying if I said you didn't still scare me. But it's fading."

Nathan fought the urge to lie down next to her. If he did, he wouldn't let her leave him until morning.

"I don't suppose you know why they worry about me?" She paused. "Didn't think so."

Just as Nathan thought his own senses were returning to normal, his animal instincts came soaring back. He could give her friends something to worry about. He could take her now. Nathan doubted he'd even have to force her. She would follow him with enough coaxing.

Her hand lifted to a gold heart around her neck.

"I thought maybe it was because of my dad, but they've been like this since before he died." His mate had felt heartache. "It's gotten worse over the years. They keep acting like I should know why, but I don't."

Nathan caved and laid down beside her, setting his head in her lap, hoping she would touch him.

"I love camping. And I look forward to this first trip of the year, but..." She sighed. "I hate to admit this, but this trip hasn't been what it should be. My friends have really pissed me off this time. And then there's you." Nathan lifted his lip and emitted a low growl. She better not say she had a problem with him. "Not like that."

He settled.

"It's just strange."

Nathan closed his eyes while Shaye continued to rub his head and she looked out over the water. Silence descended, and the first moment of peace since the turmoil that over-whelmed him two nights ago descended on him. It wouldn't last. Pain would return when he had to let her go tonight.

Taking her with him now crossed his mind again. But the last thing he wanted was for her overprotective friends to come looking for her. They wouldn't like what they found.

It was already early hours of the morning, her friends never finding their bed until well past midnight. Shaye yawned. Nathan braced himself to let her go. He nuzzled her stomach and because he could, he ran his nose along the seam of her legs until he reached the top. All he was doing was making his own torture worse, but he inhaled anyway, infusing her scent into his skin.

"Hey." She swatted his head and Nathan stopped, letting his eyes lift in a slow arch, sending her a warning. She realized her mistake, slapping a grizzly. He let the moment carry, watching her anxiety peak as she swallowed and her eyes widened, but then he continued his nuzzling how he pleased. "You're a little too friendly, big guy."

Nathan stood then nudged her shoulder to get her moving.

"What? Now you're finished with me?"

He huffed and stomped his paw on the ground toward the lake.

"Yeah, I'll come back sometime tomorrow." She touched his head and her lips softened with gratitude. "Thanks for listening."

She wrapped her arms around herself, holding her elbows, and ambled back to camp. Nathan had to look away so he didn't chase after and pull her back. His house wasn't that far away. It would be too easy to take her there and keep her. But that wouldn't be the best way to start a forced relationship.

Fucking Fate.

Nathan needed to check in with Bear, and he needed to check in with work. The job he ditched for a day with no call or explanation. He walked home, a weight with every step trying to pull him back. Bear was waiting for him in front of his house.

Where did you go?

I found my mate. I'm surprised you didn't follow me.

I didn't need to. Besides, the wind stopped me.

Fucking wind. It took Nathan considerable effort to shift. Thankfully, it wasn't as painful as the day before, but it was more than it should be. "I'm taking a shower and hopefully I'll get some sleep. See you in the morning." Bear left and Nathan went inside to shower and change his bedding before he collapsed. His sleep was a fitful one, but it was no longer haunted or impossible.

SHAYE PULLED into her driveway beside Jerry's Jeep and cut the engine. Her friends had stared at her all morning, shooting looks between them that spoke to each other and not her. Relief that the trip was over hit her with a shock. And that pissed her off all the more. Never did she feel this way when returning home from camping. Never.

She wanted to know why they treated her this way, but she didn't want to bring it up while upset. They emptied the truck and her friends followed her to her door. Yeah, they were not coming inside.

"I'm beat, guys. I'm going to have a nap so I'm not too tired for work tomorrow." She pulled on a pleasant look, the opposite of what she felt toward her friends. It saddened her she didn't feel that way toward them right now. "See you later." Shaye didn't give them a chance to let loose the arguments in their eyes, springing back and forth. She gave them a cheerful wave and went inside, locking her door behind her.

She did in fact need a nap. The trip had drained her with all the drama. After making herself lunch and showering, she curled up in bed and slept. It wasn't as restful as she hoped. Her mind wouldn't stop thinking about her three encounters with a friendly bear. Did it make her a little bit crazy that she planned to keep her promise to go back to him? Maybe. But she would do it anyway.

Shaye grabbed a few snacks on her way out the door. She locked her door, turned around, and stopped in her tracks. She had to grit her teeth. Chase walked up her driveway.

"Feeling better?" he called.

"Yeah, I am. Thanks. Did you forget something?"

"No. I just came to check up on you." He stopped at the bottom of her front steps.

"You didn't need to." She slipped her keys into her pocket and walked past him.

"Of course I did. One of us had to." Chase reached for her elbow and missed. She pretended she didn't notice.

"Well, I'm heading out. You'll have to *check up on me* another time."

"Don't be like that, Shaye."

"Never mind, Chase. See you later." She got into her truck and pulled away. Shaye vowed to deal with her friends sooner rather than later.

Shaye parked her truck next to the burned coals left from their fire. It was mid afternoon now. She had slept longer than she'd planned. Shutting the driver's door, she looked around. Nothing seemed out of place since that morning. She walked down to the lake, keeping an eye and ear around her.

"Hello?" Her soft voice carried once she broke through the trees. She didn't imagine him. But maybe that would explain her friends' worry. They saw what she didn't. She was delusional. She belonged in a thriller or horror movie.

When the bear didn't show, she sat down on the bank.

She wasn't delusional. She sighed and closed her eyes, laying back in the grass. Shaye wanted a do-over of her camping trip. She considered leaving her friends behind for the next one.

A cold wet nose on her cheek made her jump. Her eyes flew open and she gasped. The bear stood over her, his face hanging above hers. He stepped back so she could sit up.

"Hi, there. I wondered if you'd show up. I even thought I'd imagined you." Shaye reached out to run her fingers through the fur on his neck. He was a beautiful beast. "So now what?"

He nudged her shoulder a few times until she stood. Once upright, she brushed debris off her shorts and watched him as he walked toward the water. He stopped at the edge, then looked between her and the lake.

"Sorry, I didn't bring my fishing gear." He huffed and waded into the water himself. He took a drink and let the water slosh over his fur. When he looked back at her again, she could swear he was asking her to join him. "I didn't bring a swimsuit either." Shaye laughed. She took her sneakers and socks off and walked down to the edge. Sitting down, she let her feet dangle in the water. "This is the most you're getting for today. Next time I'll remember to bring more."

Shaye laughed while he played, attempting to catch fish. It shouldn't be that difficult, but she wondered if he did that on purpose, acting goofy. When he finally came out of the water, he stood away from her and shook. Shaye lifted her arm to shield herself as water droplets still reached her. Even with his fur weighted down, he was massive. The biggest grizzly she'd ever seen. Wildlife had always been a common sight with the adventures she and her dad had.

He walked over, his muscles moving with each step, and lay down beside her. He closed his eyes and looked to be enjoying the sun to dry off. Shaye pulled her feet from the water. Not that they would take long to dry. She grew more comfortable with him. She shouldn't. This was a grizzly. She could think of no logical explanation for his behavior. But she enjoyed her little secret. He showed up at the right time. When her friends were... well, she didn't know what they were doing. She needed a new friend, and he came in the form of a bear.

NATHAN CONTINUED to fight with himself on what to do about Shaye. He had been right. It was agony letting her go the night before. He spent the morning at work, not needing to fake ill for them to believe his excuse for yesterday or to allow him to leave today. He'd rather not find another job, but he didn't have a particular attachment to the one he had. If they fired him over it, it was no big deal.

But being away from her once he found her, and the fight he had with himself to go after her, left him weary. Shifters didn't get sick. Unless they'd just found their mate apparently. He couldn't do it again.

He nudged her legs before he stood. She didn't move. He pushed her again until she understood. Then he walked toward his house. When she didn't follow, he let out a groan and motioned with his head.

"Follow you?" He repeated the motion and kept walking.

After a moment, she jogged and caught up with him, lining herself beside him. Nathan allowed himself an inward grin. He knew it wouldn't have been difficult to get her to follow him. He would have happily stolen her away from her friends. Especially when she wanted to be away from them. "Where are we going?"

He looked up at her.

"Are you taking me back to your lair to feed the cubs?"

He nipped her bare thigh, barely running his sharp teeth over her skin and grunted.

"Hey!" He felt her anxiety spike for a second. "You're teasing me." She let loose a throaty, nervous laugh. "Right. You're a bear. You don't speak. How silly of me to ask."

He pushed his head under her hand and was pleased when she left it there while they walked. It took a while, but soon enough his house came into view.

"You are taking me somewhere," she whispered. When they reached the front of his house, he stepped in front of her. He pawed the ground and bobbed his head in place. He grunted and looked up to make sure she understood. "You want me to stay here." He stomped the ground once and walked around to the back of his house. After ensuring she stayed where he told her, he shifted. The pain from the day before gone. The change reverted to its normal ache and warmth.

He nodded at Bear, who lay behind the trees, then went in through his back door. He dressed quickly and took a deep breath before opening his front door. Nathan didn't have a plan in place for how to handle this. He pulled the door open and stepped out.

She turned, startled. "Uh, hi."

"Hi." His voice lowered.

"You're probably wondering what I'm doing here."

"No." He stepped down his steps. "I'm Nathan."

"Shaye." She held out her hand and he took it. He didn't shake it, only held it. Knew the same shock of heat that ran through him ran through her. He tightened his grip when she would have pulled away, letting the fever spread through both of them.

"Would you like to come in?"

"I'm not so sure about that." She frowned. "Um, have you seen a bear around here?" She tried to look around him, but she didn't go far with her hand still held in his.

"Many times," he said with a knowing tone and lift of his chin.

"So, I'm not crazy," she muttered.

"No. Come inside." He turned and placed his hand on her lower back.

"I don't know you."

"You do." Despite her frown, she walked toward the house.

"Where did the bear go?"

"He's still here." He closed the door behind him. "Want something to drink?"

"Uh, sure." Her voice was cautious, but a polite tone threaded her answer.

"Beer?" Alcohol didn't affect him, but he'd learned to like the taste. She nodded.

"Thanks." She took the bottle from him and popped it open. He was impressed with the little effort it took her to twist off the sharp cap. "Why am I in here?"

"Because I asked you." The atmosphere turned awkward quickly, but it didn't dull the heat running through Nathan. His eyes never left her while Shaye couldn't keep hers still. They darted to him, then around the room. She lifted her bottle, tilting it to the side to see the contents passed the dark glass, then took another drink. Her free hand fidgeted in her lap, fingers tapping.

He let her finish half her beer before he closed the distance between them. He set his beer down and took hers from her hand. Lifting her chin, he made sure she could see his eyes. His one distinguishing feature. She gasped, and that's when he couldn't hold back any longer.

He closed his mouth over hers, trying not to devour her in an instant. He caught her lower lip between his teeth before he soothed the nip with a swipe of his tongue. His hand moved to the back of her neck to hold her in place while his lips and tongue worked to coax her open. Every muscle in his body was taut and he had to reign himself in. He wouldn't stop and explain what was going on. He intended to take.

Her arousal rose from between her legs mixed with her sweet and spicy scent. It drove him wild and made it more difficult to hold back.

Finally, she opened and he took her mouth, running his tongue along hers in the way he planned to use her body. Her hands landed on his chest and her fingers flexed before pushing him away. With a struggle, he lifted his head, but only an inch from her mouth. He refused to put distance between him and her taste.

She panted, her breath hitting his chin. "I... You... We don't..." She stuttered, then blurted, "I need to go."

"Shh. It's okay." He couldn't offer her more. Claiming her mouth again, he moved his hands to her hips, letting his fingers dig into her flesh. He cursed the denim of her shorts for being in the way of feeling her smooth skin. And thanks to her barely-there swimsuit the day before, he knew exactly how smooth she was.

Shaye melted against him, her own desires taking over.

She pushed her hips forward and Nathan matched her movements. There was no stopping this for him. He ran his hands under the hem of her shirt and lifted. After a moment's hesitation, Shaye lifted her arms. He growled low. It rumbled up his centre. It was out of his control. He watched her eyes widen. Maybe it was recognition. He didn't know, and he didn't wait to find out. He sealed their lips while he divested her of her bra and worked on the button on her shorts.

As soon as he had her bottoms pushed down, he lifted her, her shorts falling off her ankles. He carried her to his bedroom and stopped beside the bed. She slid down his body and he let her go long enough for him to undress.

"This is not how I imagined my day going."

"My either. But I can't stop. I hope you're with me." He pulled her against him again, their skin lighting on fire as they made contact.

"Oh, I'm with you. I don't understand why, but I'm with you."

"Good. That's what I needed to hear." He kissed her and toppled them back onto his bed. His hands and his mouth turned frantic. He wasn't leaving a part of her tanned skin untouched.

He traced her faint tan lines above her breasts and enjoyed her shivers. Her flavour was infused in her skin. And he was starving.

Nathan moved his hand down her side and inward until he found her bare cunt. Fuck, she was smooth. His cock hardened. He found her clit and pulled back the hood. It was suddenly his sole purpose to feel her come apart in his arms.

He captured a nipple and suckled strongly while he worked her clit in circles with just the right amount of pressure for her to push her hips upward, reaching for more. So much arousal and heat between them that a few minutes later, she came with a gasp, silently letting go of her release.

Nathan's smile was sinful as he thought about ways to make her scream his name.

CHAPTER 5

What the hell was she doing? Shaye should leave. She never should have walked into his house. She really never should have let him hold her hand. But she couldn't stop herself. Something about him overwhelmed her and took control. God, she hoped she didn't regret this. Right now, she wasn't capable of regret.

She shivered as she came down from her orgasm, but it didn't last. Nathan's fingers probed her sensitive opening and he worked two fingers inside her. Her breath stopped, and she looked up into rich brown eyes that trapped her, embraced her like thick silk. Those eyes shocked her into remembering what she came back to the lake for.

"Stop!" His hand stopped moving, but didn't retreat. He didn't move out of the way when she tried to sit up and she bounced off his chest and moved herself on his fingers, causing her to gasp. "I abandoned the bear!"

Nathan laughed, his body shaking against hers. He started moving his fingers inside her again with shallow thrusts.

"I'm sure your bear will understand."

"How would you know? He was so demanding." He'd told her to stay in front of the house and she didn't. He would be back to look for her.

"I can be demanding." His husky voice licked flames down her body.

"I have no doubt, Nathan..."

"Proper introductions can wait. Trust me."

"Trust you? Did you just tell me to trust you?" She shouldn't trust herself at this point.

He gave her no response, no reason to trust him except to listen to her own instincts. He lowered his mouth to hers. She tried to pull away, but as soon as his lips met hers, her control vanished once again. His fingers picked up a new pace and his thumb pressed on her clit. With every part of her skin so sensitive, she barely had time to recover from the last one. And she was sure that was his purpose. He said so himself. He could be demanding. What else would he demand of her?

Shaye's climax rose with a shocking pace. Her muscles tensed and pure pleasure compiled between her legs. His mouth moved away from hers, giving her a chance to breathe. She sucked in air and moaned as his lips and teeth nipped their way down her neck. Damn, this man was pure sin.

Any man that could get a girl into bed by saying 'Hi. I'm Nathan' and handing her a beer had to be some kind of evil.

Delicious evil.

She bet he tasted delicious too.

She lost her thoughts in what he would taste like, she didn't notice him moving down her body to taste her. His tongue circled her naval and she gasped. She lost her breath entirely when his mouth replaced his thumb. Such purposeful movements with his tongue had her climbing the peak faster than ever.

Despite her best efforts, a soft cry escaped when her core reached its peak and flew over the edge in the most sensational orgasm she had to date.

"Mmm. Much better." He hummed against her clit, sending a new shock through her.

Shaye tried to muster the energy to return the favour. Not much of a favour when she selfishly craved him. She didn't have time to enact her own desires before he reared up over her and lined up his cock.

"I hope you're ready, sweetness."

She was.

He lifted one of her legs and tilted her hips toward the ceiling. He thrust in, slow and powerful, not halting when she gasped and pulled back from the deep penetration. Nathan grabbed one of her shoulders and held her in place. Her moans turned to cries, but it didn't mean she wanted this to end. The mild pain increased the pleasure. She'd never been taken like this before.

This was a mutual exchange, but Shaye lost her control. To be taken by a complete stranger... Her thoughts trailed away. The only explanation was insanity. A friendship with a bear and an affair with a stranger. Maybe she should allow her friends to worry about her.

"Your mind wanders easily," Nathan lowered his voice to pull her attention back.

"Sex with a stranger gives a girl a lot to think about."

"Stop thinking." He punctuated his command with grinding against her clit, sending a wave up her stomach and back down to her core, like the carnival ride that propels the riders into the air before plummeting to the ground.

"Okay." Shaye whimpered. His hand left her shoulder and moved down her chest. She loved having her breasts played with, but beyond the initial fondle, no man had been interested. Nathan rounded on her nipples and rolled them between his fingers. He knew how to use them.

Electrical zings shot from his fingers to her clit and she arched her back. She let out a soft moan and Nathan switched to her other nipple until she did the same thing. She wasn't sure how much longer she could last. Everything in her tightened. She needed release.

She tried to move her hand down her body to touch her clit, but he grasped her wrist. His fingers flexed, and he pulled her hand upward above her head.

"Mine." The possessive undertone surprised her. But she obeyed and left her hand there when he let go and moved his fingers in the direction hers had been heading.

One touch. One circle. And hundreds of pleasurable shocks struck out and spread through her body. Her muscles tightened and her hips bucked. She let out a silent scream. Sound tried to escape her, but she had no air to use since Nathan stole it all.

His teeth grazed the column of her neck as his hips pounded into her. Only moments before he spilled inside her, he pulled his face up and sealed their lips together. Fresh spasms started, and she moaned into his mouth.

Shaye collapsed beneath him, her eyes closing, as he pulled out of her. She winced at the loss. It wasn't long until the bed dipped with his return, but she was already half asleep, worrying about herself and her bear.

Nathan shuddered as he pulled out. It wasn't enough. The urge to have more of her came soaring back. But he wore the poor girl out. What a fucking idiot. He invited her in and fucked her, taking advantage of the attraction the mate bond created. He didn't give her a chance to get to know him and decide for herself.

At least he kept himself from biting her. Asher's *shifter club* turned out useful to him. He wouldn't have bothered resisting the urge to mark her if it weren't for the knowledge they gave.

He pulled her into his arms and waited for her to wake. Now that he had her, he could slow things down. He rolled his eyes as he lied to himself. Nothing would move slow from here. But he had a dilemma. She expected to see a bear.

He didn't think he could tell her so soon. Which meant he had to play a double life with her. A double lie.

Her muscles tensed under his arm, but she stayed still.

"I should apologize." His voice rumbled in the quiet of the room.

"Please, don't."

"I wasn't going to. I should, but I can't."

Shaye pushed back and he allowed the distance. She sat herself up on her elbow and he moved his arm behind his head. "I feel the same. I should regret doing that, but I don't." She took in a breath, forcing her breasts to rise, and Nathan wasn't gentlemen enough not to look. "What do we do now?"

Nathan knew what he wanted, what he needed, but he wouldn't take advantage of her again. He looked at the clock on his nightstand. "We get dinner." He gave her a lazy smile, attempting to flirt, to draw her in.

"Just like that?"

"Well, we skipped a few steps. Maybe we should go back and check them off."

"You have a strange way of asking a girl out." Nathan sensed her nerves, but at least she flashed him flirty eyes.

"I didn't ask." He raised a brow.

She paused with a twist on her lips. "Sure. Why not?" Shaye pushed the blanket off and tried to climb over him to get out of bed. His hand clasped her waist and flattened her on top of him. He lifted his head and captured her lips. She opened, and Nathan savoured her taste before letting her go. Shaye stood by the bed, and he kept a hand on her hip to steady her. "This isn't fair. Your clothes are in here, but you left mine out there."

"Are you modest?" He swung his legs over the edge of the bed. She smirked and lifted her chin.

"No." Then she walked out of his room with a delicious sway to her round ass. He was still grinning while he buttoned his jeans. She walked back in, all dressed, before he found his shirt. Her eyes roamed down his chest and her tongue slid over her lips.

"Careful where your eyes go, sweetness. I might forget I'm hungry." Her gaze snapped back up, but she tore her eyes away as her cheeks glowed a dusky rose under her tanned skin. "What do you like to eat?"

"I'm not picky."

"Great. Let's go." He led her out of the house with a hand on her lower back. As soon as he shut his front door, she stopped and looked around, searching the trees.

"Where did he go?"

"Your bear?"

"Yes, *the* bear." She used the word to distance herself, refusing to admit to a connection to the wild, and danger-ous, animal.

"I'm sure he's fine."

"But he told me to stay here and I didn't. What if he's looking for me? Or what if he doesn't come back?" He felt her worry.

"He told you?"

Her eyes narrowed. "You said I wasn't crazy."

"Would you like to wait for him?" What the hell was he doing? They'd be standing there forever. He couldn't run back and forth each time she wanted to see Nathan the man or Nathan the bear. She chewed on her cheek.

"No. I'm being silly. And you are too. Offering to wait for a bear to come back."

"You'll find him again. I promise." He took her hand and pulled her toward his truck.

"How can you promise something like that?"

"Because that's a promise I can make." He would have a very thin line to tread with her until he was ready to tell her what he was. He opened the passenger door for her and helped her in, then made his way around to the driver's side. Once he started the truck, she turned in her seat.

"Now that we aren't busy, think we could have proper introductions?"

"Marks."

"It's nice to meet you, Mr. Marks." Polite mock formality enunciated each word. "I'm Shaye Tierney. And what do you do?"

"I work at the lumber yard."

"I assume that house is yours."

"Yes, it is." He sent a side glance. "And you?"

"I'm a realtor's assistant."

"You live in Alder Ridge?" He wasn't sure how he missed her if she did.

"Yeah." Because he hadn't been meant to be. Until now. Fucking Fate.

"So, what were you doing in my woods?"

"*Your* woods?" Shaye scoffed and tilted her head sideways, her eyes widening as if to say he had some nerve.

"Yeah, my woods." Nathan hid his grin with authority, staking his claim.

"I'll have you know, I've been camping at the lake since I was a child. Although rarely the same area twice. But I've been coming to *your* woods for years. This was the first year I ever camped on that side."

Nathan spent so much of his time around that lake since he was a cub.

Letting the thought go, he pulled into the pub and parked his truck.

"I love this place." So did Nathan.

"Their burgers are the best."

"No way!" Shaye twisted in her seat with her fierce denial. "Jackie's on the other side of town has the best." She scrunched her nose and gave a half shrug. "These guys are close, though."

"You are wrong."

She laughed. "I always order the appetizer platter here. A little bit of everything."

They hopped out of the truck and met at the front. Nathan didn't keep his distance or keep his hands off her. He wrapped one arm around her and pulled her forward. He kissed her, deep, overwhelming both of their senses. When he finally released her, he didn't let her go. He held her body against his, ensuring the heat rushed through them.

Reluctantly, he softened his grip for her to step back. When she stopped wobbling forward, he pulled his arm back and let his hand rest on her hip. He better get them well acquainted soon.

SHAYE ALLOWED herself to let go of her thoughts on being delusional. Even sitting across from Nathan in a pub, her mood was similar to what it was at the lake. There was something about Nathan. Arrogance. That was it. Arrogant and wild. It had to be the wild that drew her to him.

No. Shut that thought the fuck up, Shaye. She wasn't going crazy. Even if she'd slept with a man she knew for only five minutes.

She looked up from her plate and saw humour hovering around his lips.

"Am I amusing?" she asked.

"Your thoughts are written all over your face, but they keep changing." He took a bite of his burger.

"Guess I should never play poker."

"You'd just need to practice."

"Do you play?" He'd be good at it if he did.

"I can." That would be a no.

"I don't often have time for much other than work. I schedule vacation just to go camping in my home town. Today is still a vacation day. I'm back at it bright and early tomorrow. Way too early."

"You sound like you don't like your job." He set his burger down to eat some fries.

"I do, most of the time. I'm good at it, and I think there's always enjoyment in something you're good at. It's an accomplishment. I think it's in our nature to seek validation, which brings enjoyment."

He didn't look like he agreed. It was the first time he looked away from her and focused on his food.

"Shaye?" Shaye looked up and saw Jenna and Jerry. Jerry had his arm around her shoulders just like teenagers, despite the fact they hadn't been teenagers for years.

"Hi, guys." If they weren't scowling at her instead of looking happy to see her, she wouldn't have had to pretend to be happy to see them.

"Chase said he stopped by earlier." Jerry said.

"He did." Shaye chanced a sideways glance at Nathan across the table. He'd put his food down and leaned back in his seat. His face was flat and unreadable, but somehow his eyes narrowed without thinning. There was caution toward her friends. With an inward shrug from his odd reaction, Shaye moved her attention back to Jenna and Jerry. "I didn't have time to hang out with him. I was heading out when he showed up."

"Yeah, he said that," Jerry intoned with a clear accusation toward Shaye.

"So, who's this?" Jenna didn't mask her suspicions with a happy tone. Shaye knew her too well for her to bother.

"This is Nathan." She shifted her gaze across the table. "Nathan, these are friends of mine, Jenna and Jerry."

"Best friends." Jenna corrected. "Nice to meet you." Jerry held out his hand and Nathan politely shook it, despite his stiff posture. Maybe he just didn't like interruptions. "If we had known you were coming out to eat, we would have waited for you, Shaye."

"I didn't know I was coming. It's okay."

Jenna pushed off of Jerry, breaking away from his hold to bend down and hug Shaye. Shaye's arms jerked upward and froze in the air. The sudden affection was out of place. She let her arms fall on her friend's back and gave her an uncertain pat. "Call me as soon as you get home. I mean it." Jenna whispered in her ear.

Jenna pulled away and she and Jerry left to sit, choosing a table with a straight line of sight to her and Nathan.

Embarrassment flooded her cheeks. Shaye felt like a child caught sneaking out past curfew. As the warmth spread, she refused to meet Nathan's eyes. It would be entirely obvious to him.

Shaye allowed herself to let go of her thoughts on being delusional. Even sitting across from Nathan in a pub, her mood was similar to what it was at the lake. There was something about Nathan. Arrogance. That was it. Arrogant and wild. It had to be the wild that drew her to him.

No. Shut that thought the fuck up, Shaye. She wasn't going crazy. Even if she'd slept with a man she knew for only five minutes.

She looked up from her plate and saw humour hovering around his lips.

"Am I amusing?" she asked.

"Your thoughts are written all over your face, but they keep changing." He took a bite of his burger.

"Guess I should never play poker."

"You'd just need to practice."

"Do you play?" He'd be good at it if he did.

"I can." That would be a no.

"I don't often have time for much other than work. I schedule vacation just to go camping in my home town. Today is still a vacation day. I'm back at it bright and early tomorrow. Way too early."

"You sound like you don't like your job." He set his burger down to eat some fries.

"I do, most of the time. I'm good at it, and I think there's always enjoyment in something you're good at. It's an accomplishment. I think it's in our nature to seek validation, which brings enjoyment."

He didn't look like he agreed. It was the first time he looked away from her and focused on his food.

"Shaye?" Shaye looked up and saw Jenna and Jerry. Jerry had his arm around her shoulders just like teenagers, despite the fact they hadn't been teenagers for years.

"Hi, guys." If they weren't scowling at her instead of looking happy to see her, she wouldn't have had to pretend to be happy to see them.

"Chase said he stopped by earlier." Jerry said.

"He did." Shaye chanced a sideways glance at Nathan across the table. He'd put his food down and leaned back in his seat. His face was flat and unreadable, but somehow his eyes narrowed without thinning. There was caution toward her friends. With an inward shrug from his odd reaction, Shaye moved her attention back to Jenna and Jerry. "I didn't have time to hang out with him. I was heading out when he showed up."

"Yeah, he said that," Jerry intoned with a clear accusation toward Shaye.

"So, who's this?" Jenna didn't mask her suspicions. Shaye knew her too well for her to bother.

"This is Nathan." She shifted her gaze across the table. "Nathan, these are friends of mine, Jenna and Jerry."

"Best friends." Jenna corrected. "Nice to meet you." Jerry held out his hand and Nathan politely shook it, despite his stiff posture. Maybe he just didn't like interruptions. "If we had known you were coming out to eat, we would have waited for you, Shaye."

"I didn't know I was coming. It's okay."

Jenna pushed off of Jerry, breaking away from his hold to bend down and hug Shaye. Shaye's arms jerked upward and froze in the air. The sudden affection was out of place. She let her arms fall on her friend's back and gave her an uncertain pat. "Call me as soon as you get home. I mean it." Jenna whispered in her ear.

Jenna pulled away and she and Jerry left to sit, choosing a table with a straight line of sight to her and Nathan.

Embarrassment flooded her cheeks. Shaye felt like a child caught sneaking out past curfew. As the warmth spread, she refused to meet Nathan's eyes. It would be entirely obvious to him.

"Shaye." His deep voice somehow sounded soft.

"Hmm?" She tilted her face, but kept her attention on the last of her food.

"Shaye." She allowed a tentative look up, not spending time for her eyes to linger. "Shaye." Denying him a third time was impossible. A moment of irrational anger flashed in his eyes, changing the colour to a richer brown. They trapped her as they simmered through emotions until they mirrored her own with understanding. "Do you want to go?" With his eyes so focused, he saw her distress. His tender voice was a surprise. He was giving her a choice to step away.

She nodded and finished her drink while he hailed the waiter to get the bill. He gave her his credit card and they left as soon as he got the receipt. Shaye didn't look at Jenna and Jerry. She was sure they were watching, and she would not let them see her embarrassment, giving them validation for their worry.

Nathan led her out the door and to his truck with a hand on the back of her neck. It was heavy and hot, possessive and caring. He drove them back to his place in silence. Something Shaye appreciated.

When he approached the lake, he asked, "Where did you park?"

"That way." She pointed in the direction of her truck.

"Nice truck." Shaye loved the envy she heard in his voice.

"Thanks."

After he parked, he met her at the driver's side of her truck. "Do you want to talk about what upset you at the pub?"

"No." She shook her head and firmed her mouth. "But it's something I will deal with very soon."

He took a couple steps closer. "You can spend the night." He lifted his hand and traced his fingers along her jaw. Her pulse raced from the simple touch.

"I could," she said on a wishful breath, "but I should go home."

"You should." He closed the remaining gap and his hand delved into her hair.

"I'm going to."

"Good."

Nathan bent his head and captured her mouth. She couldn't breathe and didn't want to. She matched every move and every stroke, but pulled away when reality crashed back into her mind. "I'm going to go home now."

His mouth cracked as his lips twitched. "Okay." He stepped back. "Will you come back tomorrow?"

"I don't know. Maybe."

"Good enough. Take care, Shaye."

He walked back to his truck, but didn't get in until Shaye climbed into hers. He backed out and she followed, waving when she passed him to go home and he turned to go further up the road toward his house.

She might have told him maybe, but she knew she

would return. For Nathan and the bear. "Shaye." His deep voice somehow sounded soft.

"Hmm?" She let her face tilt, but kept her attention on the last of her food.

"Shaye." She allowed a tentative look up, not spending time for her eyes to linger. "Shaye." Denying him a third time was impossible. A moment of irrational anger flashed in his eyes, changing the colour to a richer brown. They trapped her as they simmered through emotions until they mirrored her own with understanding. "Do you want to go?" With his eyes so focused, he saw her distress. His tender voice was a surprise. He was giving her a choice to step away.

She nodded and finished her drink while he hailed the waiter to get the bill. He gave her his credit card and they left as soon as he got the receipt. Shaye didn't look at Jenna and Jerry. She was sure they were watching, and she would not let them see her embarrassment, giving them validation for their worry.

Nathan led her out the door and to his truck with a hand on the back of her neck. It was heavy and hot, possessive and caring. He drove them back to his place in silence. Something Shaye appreciated.

When he approached the lake, he asked, "Where did you park?"

"That way." She pointed in the direction of her truck.

"Nice truck." Shaye loved the envy she heard in his voice.

"Thanks."

After he parked, he met her at the driver's side of her truck. "Do you want to talk about what upset you at the pub?"

"No." She shook her head and firmed her mouth. "But it's something I will deal with very soon."

He took a couple steps closer. "You can spend the night." He lifted his hand and traced his fingers along her jaw. Her pulse raced from the simple touch.

"I could," she said on a wishful breath, "but I should go home."

"You should." He closed the remaining gap and his hand delved into her hair.

"I'm going to."

"Good."

Nathan bent his head and captured her mouth. She couldn't breathe and didn't want to. She matched every move and every stroke, but pulled away when reality crashed back into her mind. "I'm going to go home now."

His mouth cracked as his lips twitched. "Okay." He stepped back. "Will you come back tomorrow?"

"I don't know. Maybe."

"Good enough. Take care, Shaye."

He walked back to his truck, but didn't get in until Shaye climbed into hers. He backed out and she followed, waving when she passed him to go home and he turned to go further up the road toward his house.

She might have told him maybe, but she knew she would return. For Nathan and the bear.

CHAPTER 6

Shaye pulled her cell from her nightstand and called Jenna when she got home. She didn't want to, but the alternative of her friends nagging her left her no choice. "Hi, Jenna. I'm home."

"Who the hell was that, Shaye?" Shaye had to pull the phone away from her ear. Jenna's lack of greeting created fresh anger. "How come we've never met him before you went on a date?"

"Excuse me?" Shaye froze in place on her way to the kitchen with Jenna's accusation. "Since when do I have to run my dates by you guys first?" Shaye had been on plenty of dates without the approval of her friends.

"You don't," she hedged. "It's just..."

"You're worried about me." Shaye finished for her. "Yeah, I know. You've all said. But what you haven't said is why. And every time I ask, you all act as if it's obvious. So maybe it's time for you to spill."

"You seriously don't know?"

"No!" she snapped.

"Oh my God, Shaye." Silence followed Jenna's shock and

Shaye's patience no longer worked. She hung up, not caring for the first time that she cut off her best friend.

After getting some water, she showered and got ready for bed. The light on her phone blinked, and it stopped her from getting into bed. Missed messages, phone calls, and voicemails. She didn't bother listening to her voicemail, but there were messages and phone calls from Jenna, Jerry, and Chase. Shaye sighed and turned off her phone. She didn't need it until her scheduled vacation was over, anyway.

The next day, her ever demanding boss kept her busy enough that she couldn't even think about her friends, let alone return their messages. By lunch, she had to call each of them to tell them to stop. Their constant messages interfered with her job, popping up in the middle of tasks or when talking with clients. They cajoled her to talk to them, but she'd cut them off and hang up.

Mental exhaustion started a pounding behind her eyes as she pulled into her driveway. Any strength she might have had left vanished as Jerry's blue jeep pulled up behind her truck, blocking her in. All three of her friends got out and Chase carried a couple pizza boxes. They all walked toward her laughing, as if it was any other night.

"Pizza and beer. Best way to end the day." Chase stood beside her wearing a goofy grin. They all waited for her to unlock her door. Without her energy, Shaye let them in. They piled into her living room. Jenna fetched plates from the kitchen and they dished everyone up, even leaving a space for Shaye to sit beside Jenna on her couch.

On her dad's couch. In her dad's house. All hers since he passed. It was home, but it was a home with a missing piece. Him. Why hadn't she noticed that before? Her friends. They always filled up the space, blocking the gaping hole in the structure that should be her dad.

She stared at all of them while they shoved their mouths full of pizza and Jerry flicked through the channels on her TV.

"Is this all because my dad is gone?"

"What are you talking about?" asked Chase, not sparing her more than a second's glance.

"Now who's being dense," she said under her breath. Not that she thought they didn't hear her. She didn't care if they did anymore. "The worrying, the checking up on me, the showing up uninvited?"

"Shaye, we know you made peace with your dad's death, but we're always here for you." Jenna reached over and laid her hand on Shaye's.

"So that is what this is about?"

All three of her friends looked away. Jenna chewed her cheek and the guys pursed their lips to lock in the words. But all three had the same look in their eyes. Sympathy and guilt. Shaye waited, and the silence grew.

"Is it such a bad thing that your friends care enough about you to worry?"

"When those friends treat me like a child who's broken the rules, like someone who might explode at any moment, or like someone who isn't capable of taking care of themselves? Yes. Which you all know damn well I'm more capable than any of you." Her last words were hurtful, but she wouldn't hold back the truth when that's what she wanted from them. This house hadn't been mortgage free when her dad passed. It was now. There'd been repairs needed that her dad never finished. They were complete now. She had a job, a home, independence. There was nothing wrong with where her friends were in their lives, but it wasn't where she was. She was proud of herself, and she knew her dad would be proud of her too.

"Shaye, let's just have a nice night." Jerry pulled out another slice of pizza and the others followed suit to move on with a *nice night*.

"You won't tell me, will you?"

"It's not so easy." Jenna paused and worked her lower lip between her teeth before her mouth worked up and down. Shaye tensed, waiting for the words to finally spill from her friend. "It's your mom, Shaye. You know." Jenna tilted her head, then went back to her pizza while everyone ignored her, the guys talking about a mutual friend who'd landed a job as a bouncer at their favourite club.

Shaye's confusion grew. Her mom died when Shaye had been a baby. Whatever their reason, it was an uncomfortable topic for them.

Feeling suffocated, Shaye decided to leave. "Jerry, can you move your Jeep, please?"

"Why?"

"I'm leaving. You guys do what you want, stay or don't stay, but I have other plans."

"You suddenly have plans now?" Skepticism dripped from his features as he called her out on her lie.

"You never asked if I was free before you all barged into my house and took over. Move your Jeep or I'll run it over." Shaye would regret her rudeness later, but they were leaving her no choice. They wouldn't talk and she needed out.

"Jesus, Shaye." Jerry glared, but at least he stood and walked out the door. She grabbed her bag and followed him out. She was in her truck before he got out of his Jeep after parking it on the street.

He stood in front of it with his arms crossed. His jaw locked and nostrils flared, and he shook his head at her as she drove away.

She forced her mind to blank, thinking of nothing, while

she drove, but the first tear escaped as she parked in front of Nathan's.

What was she doing here? She couldn't go crying to a man she just met. She got out of the truck and started for the lake to find some peace. When she finished crying, she'd find her peace there.

NATHAN STOOD INSIDE HIS HOUSE, spying through the window, and watched his mate swipe at her cheek as she walked toward the lake. She might not be coming to him, but she came back. Nathan stripped and left his clothes by his back door. He shifted, the ache less now that his mate was near. Following her through the woods, he heard her tiny sniffles. He wanted to know who hurt his mate. Although, he could guess.

He allowed his paws to crunch twigs and leaves on the ground so he didn't scare her. He found her sitting by the lake. She turned when he approached.

"It's you." She wiped all of her tears away. An attempt to hide her pain even from a bear. He lay down and rested his head on her lap. "I'm sorry I left yesterday." Nathan wiggled his head. "I really haven't had a great day."

He lifted his head and looked directly at her, willing her to talk to him. He didn't care if she talked to the bear or the man. They were the same and eventually she would learn to trust both.

"It's my friends. I still don't understand, but at least they told me it's because of my mom. But that doesn't make sense to me either. They're acting as if the subject is uncomfortable for them. I left. They all showed up at my place like any other night after they've been hovering and nagging for two days. I couldn't pretend things were normal when they've been treating me like I'm going to break. Then they get mad when I lash out and leave. God, you should have seen the look on Jerry's face."

He touched his nose to hers, not knowing anything better to give her for comfort, and to at least make her smile.

"They caught me with Nathan yesterday. Caught, like a teenager who snuck out her bedroom window. I was so embarrassed. I did nothing wrong, but if you ask them, I did. Speaking of Nathan. Is he why you took me to that house yesterday?" Nathan tilted his head. "Right, you can't answer."

Nathan didn't have to know her well to understand that out here is where she felt free. In the short time she'd been here, her entire mood changed. The more she talked, the more her voice lightened.

Her phone went off in her bag. He moved his head out of the way so she had access to it.

"Messages from Jenna. But also work. I'm ignoring Jenna. I can't ignore work though." Her attention moved to her phone and Nathan waited. She finished with a sigh and was about to put her phone away when it rang. Shaye stared at the screen until he was sure the call was about to end, then answered at the last second. She didn't even finish saying hello before Jenna started in.

"Where are you?"

"It doesn't matter. Look, Jenna. You're my best friend. If anyone can tell me what you all have in your heads, it's you. But you refused. You're all smothering me when you know I'm fine. So, tell me or leave me alone."

"Where are you? We'll come get you. We can talk." Her tone took a one eighty turn from accusatory to placating.

"Not tonight, Jenna. If you're ready to tell me what it is,

you can come to my place tomorrow after work. Alone." Shaye hung up. Her fingers squeezed her phone, but she was slow setting it down. Her air pushed out of her nose with the motion.

As much as his anger grew at her friends, Nathan was proud of Shaye. She wasn't letting them walk over her.

She lay back in the grass as the sun started to set and Nathan let her be for a while, but he wanted her back at his place. Eventually, he nudged her to sit up.

"Look at the sky. It's beautiful. The light shining between the trees, shimmering strips on the water. You probably see this every day." She wrapped an arm around his neck. They watched the sun set a little further before Nathan's patience fled.

He pushed up and nudged her to do the same.

"We going somewhere?"

He walked off toward his house and she followed.

"You're taking me back to Nathan's, aren't you?" He didn't acknowledge her. "Please tell me I can trust him. I don't know him at all, but I can't seem to help myself. The last thing I want is for my friends to have a genuine reason to worry."

Nathan stopped and turned to face her. He had no way to tell her to trust him, but he hoped she understood when he nuzzled her stomach and hip, pushing his head under her hand.

"I hope that's a yes. He was good to me yesterday." They kept walking, her hand resting on his back. When they reached his house, he stopped and stomped the ground. "Okay," she said, amusement playing on her lips.

He left her and shifted behind his house. He dressed before walking through the house to open the front door. Shaye was on her way up the steps when he swung it open.

"I was hoping you'd come back." He held the door wider with his arm near the top and she walked in, ducking her head even though she didn't come close to touching his arm.

"Me too."

"What brought you back?" Nathan would tire of a double life soon. He didn't like putting on an ignorant act.

"I wanted to." She took in a breath. "And I had a bad day."

"Have you eaten?" She shook her head. "Good. You can tell me about it while we eat." Nathan made them sandwiches and listened to a summed-up version of what she said at the lake, but it surprised him she kept going.

"I'm more capable of taking care of myself than any of them. I don't understand what my parents have to do with this."

"What happened to them?" Her hand reached up to the gold heart on her neck. It must have been from her father. All Nathan got from his father was poverty and boxes full of crap.

"My dad died in a car accident shortly after I graduated high school." Her voice was soft. She still carried her pain. But she also carried strength. Nathan would bet her father gave her that too.

"And your mom?" Her hand dropped. She didn't hold the same emotion to both parents. Neither did Nathan.

"She had postpartum depression a few months after I was born. She," she pursed her lips and looked at him for a brief moment. "She took her life."

"I'm sorry." And because her vulnerability exposed his, he said, "I lost my mother when I was very young."

"What happened?"

Nathan shook his head. "Another time." He wouldn't divulge those gruesome details, not yet. Maybe never.

"Your dad?"

"I don't remember him, and I've never found out what happened to him." Once he got older, he searched the boxes left in their tiny shack of a home. There wasn't much to find. At least not much of which he could make sense. Clothes, knick knacks, papers. He found his birth certificate and other documents he needed when he'd turned eighteen. But he never found out what happened to his dad. As far as Nathan knew, he'd abandoned them. Nathan may never find out. He may never know why his mother had been killed.

Her hand covered his and she squeezed.

It only took that touch to send heat through him, through both of them. He heard her breath quicken. But he promised himself he wouldn't take advantage of the attraction again. Not without talking first.

"What brought you back here, Shaye?"

"I'm not entirely sure. Yesterday was..." She trailed off. "You seemed to understand what I needed. Not just here at your place," her cheeks changed colour to a light red, "but at the pub too."

That was enough for Nathan. She wanted to be here, and she came to him on her own. She was his.

MAYBE SHE SHOULDN'T HAVE COME HERE. She should probably leave. This was irresponsible. But the last thing Shaye wanted was to return home to find her friends still there waiting for her.

She looked at Nathan. His short brown hair, bright brown eyes, and every single muscle in his body with definition, pulled her toward him. It was a stronger physical attraction than she'd ever felt before, but there was more. Something more connected them.

Okay, Shaye. What are you going to do? She wouldn't leave. Shaye stood from the table and made the move neither of them seemed ready to make. Nathan turned his chair out to meet her. She carefully settled herself in his lap.

"Nathan? Can you explain what this is between us?"

"I can." He paused. "Do you believe in Fate?"

"Not really." If Fate was real, then She was cruel.

"Neither did I." He pulled her down and sealed their lips. Shaye let herself get lost in him. She came back for an escape, so she was going to take it.

He stood, lifting her into the air. Shaye tightened her arms around his neck until he let her down beside his bed.

"Shaye, there's more I should tell you." He blinked and the muscles around his lips twitched with the struggle to say what he wanted. "But it's too soon. And it isn't so simple." The similar words spoken by her friends doused the heat running through her veins. She stepped back. His jaw worked up and down, trying to form words, but he stayed silent.

"I'm going to go."

"I'm sorry." He reached out and cupped her jaw. Shaye didn't have the power to pull away. She loved his touch. "Please stay. I swear it will make sense soon."

"I can't. Things aren't that complicated. *It isn't so simple* doesn't work for me." She didn't stop him when he pulled her back. He kissed her. Gentle, but raw. He let her go.

"Can I get your number? I want to see you again."

"Sure." Shaye shrugged and agreed, because she wanted to see him too. She jotted out her phone numbers, cell and home, on a piece of paper on his nightstand.

After one last look at each other, she left. She had to

hurry, so she didn't get pulled back. His eyes alone could do it, but if he touched her again, she was certain she would cave.

She looked around for the bear before getting in her truck. He really was bringing her to Nathan. Sneaky bear.

Relief was sweet when she saw Jerry's jeep was no longer parked outside her house. She felt a fresh wave of fatigue as she locked her door behind her.

"Shaye?" Shaye screamed and whirled around. Jenna sat up on the couch, a blanket around her shoulders.

"Jenna. You're still here?"

"Yeah."

"Were you waiting for me so you could tell me what's going on?"

"I'm sorry, Shaye. We all are. It's just," Jenna hesitated and shrugged, "your mom was the same age you are now."

"That's it? What my mom went through doesn't even apply to me right now. You guys have been watching me like a hawk, thinking I'll get depression and attempt suicide?"

"That's not such a big leap, Shaye. Your dad told you she had battled depression before she had you. You went through a lot losing your dad. And you've been dragging us out to camp more every year since he passed." Jenna let the blanket fall and stood up.

"Yes, it is a big leap, Jenna. I didn't know my mom, and neither did any of you. We have no way to know what happened or why, or what was going through her mind, and to assume I'll repeat her actions due to some genetic predisposition is unfair. To myself and my mom. You've all been me treating like a child who can't take care of herself. That's enough. It ends now."

"All right." Jenna threw her hands in the air. "We'll stop. But you better damn well come to us if you need anything."

"Jenna, we've been through so much and I wouldn't have made it this far without you." Shaye softened, but the argument drained her of anything she had left.

"Where did you go?"

"Back to the lake." She didn't want to tell her about Nathan. Not after how she acted at the pub.

"Who was that guy yesterday?" She spoke with the same judgmental undertone.

"Just a guy, Jenna." Shaye sighed, trying to rid herself of the frustrations the drama had caused. "You can sleep on the couch if you want, if Jerry isn't coming back to get you."

"Thanks, but I think it's best if I call him."

"Suit yourself."

"Shaye?" Shaye stopped at the bottom of the stairs and turned only her head and one shoulder. "We good?"

Shaye nodded. "Yeah, we're good." She went to bed, taking the steps slowly, trying not to run away from her friend. She left Jenna to let herself out, not caring about locking the door behind her. Space might be good for Shaye and her friends.

CHAPTER 7

Nathan arrived early at Asher's. Asher wanted to show off the work he'd done to the building and ask for suggestions before the project went too far. He'd liked Nathan's changes, when he'd ordered the lumber. Asher and Gwen stepped out of their house, and Zachary had just arrived and got off his bike.

"Hey." Asher nodded at Nathan. "Everything okay with you?"

"Yeah."

"Ever figure out what the wind wanted?" All eyes turned on him, eager for information.

"I did."

"And?" Gwen asked. She hiked her backpack higher on her shoulders. He looked at the three pairs of eyes pinning him in place, feeling cornered, like the foxes he and Bear had chased for fun as cubs. They'd watch just to see what the smaller animals did when stuck.

It wasn't any of their business, despite that this was the purpose of their group. But was Nathan ready to admit he'd found his mate? He recognized her as his.

"I'll tell you later. Let's get going." He started off for the trees and waited for them to follow. The three shifters ditched their clothes and shifted, bones popped and colourful magic winds flowed. He'd never seen anyone shift until he'd met Asher and Zachary. He saw what it looked like for the wolves and assumed it was similar for him.

Gwen climbed onto Asher's back and they started off on a run to the work site, all three animal pairs joining them along the way. Bear sidled up beside him and Nathan bumped their shoulders. Bear bumped him back and they took up the rear of the group.

They stopped once to rest and give Gwen time to stretch. Nathan and Bear hung back from the group. Both fine being left alone. He knew the benefits of this group and that he should at least attempt to be friendly, but friendly wasn't his nature. He'd been raised as a bear. His interest in other beings had only been out of necessity. It took some time as a human to remember how to act around others. The memories he had were of a four-year-old boy. They weren't helpful. It was easy for him to revert to being quiet and alone.

Asher and Zachary strode over, leaving Gwen with Kai and Smoke. They said nothing. Two sets of shining eyes attempted to look through him. Nathan cringed as he prepared to share something personal.

I found my mate.

Seriously? Asked Asher, eagerness pitching in his deep echoed voice.

Yeah, but she knows nothing of what I am yet.

When are you going to tell her? Zachary stepped closer.

Soon. He wouldn't share her problems with them. She didn't like secrets that involved her. Nathan wouldn't be able to keep this from her if he wanted to claim her. One more date and he would take her back to the lake and show her.

You seem calm for having recently found your mate. I wasn't calm until I marked Gwen.

I'm not calm. His senses burned when she wasn't near him.

You hide it well, said Zachary. Nathan shrugged. Maybe his wild outburst when he first discovered her helped to keep control of himself now. That he already had her in his bed didn't hurt either.

"Everyone ready?" Gwen called.

Let's go. They followed Asher. Gwen sat on Kai's back, and they set off again. When they reached the site, Kai let Gwen off and he and Smoke broke away to check in with the pack and Bear wandered off on his own to explore.

They all shifted. Asher tossed each of them a pair of pants from a bag beside the pile of lumber.

Asher walked them through the foundation. "There will be a decent kitchen. Nothing special, but enough room to cook and a bit of storage that we'll keep stocked. A common living space here." He held his hands outward from the kitchen. "Two bathrooms, and the rest of the rooms are bedrooms. Six for now. But thanks to Nathan's suggestion, we'll be able to build onto this structure if we find we need more rooms."

Nathan knew what Asher planned with this group, but the success of it was uncertain. If successful, he would need the space. Or he'd have to build a second building.

"This looks good, Asher." Zachary walked along what would be the walls. "I think this is a good thing. What do you think, Nathan?"

Nathan had given little of his opinion of Asher's plans. Other than showing up, he didn't give them any other indication he cared.

"It's good."

"Think you'll ever use it?"

"Maybe. If I can't get across town. I live in the woods near the lake on the opposite side. Lots of privacy. I've grown up with a place like this." That was the most personal information he'd ever spoken. It was the only reason they would look at him with shocked, wide eyes.

"Okay then. Glad to hear it." Asher cleared his throat and started talking about the surrounding land. Nathan followed, but his attention wavered. He wanted to call Shaye. He needed to see her and make this right.

SHAYE HADN'T SEEN her friends for three days. She thought maybe she should call them, but she struggled with reaching out. After talking to Jenna, Shaye knew they would still worry. She didn't want to call them until she thought they would trust her.

The calls from Nathan each night pulled her closer to him and made ignoring her friends a little easier. He didn't say much, but he was a good listener. He listened to the troubles of her day. And at the end of each call, he asked her to come back. She told him she'd think about it. And she hadn't stopped.

Shaye finally left work, but it was late and her stomach threw a tantrum. Her thumb hovered over Nathan's name on her phone. She closed her eyes and pressed the button to call. One ring and he answered.

"Shaye." Her name sounded through the speaker like an eager prayer.

"Have you eaten? I know it's late." Shaye blurted out her invite instead of saying hello.

"I can always eat."

She laughed. "I'm starving. Meet me at Jackie's?"

"I'll be there soon."

Shaye pulled out of the office parking lot and arrived at Jackie's before him. Inside, she got a table and couldn't wait for Nathan to order. She started with an appetizer and drinks, assuming he'd be fine with a beer. He sat down just as the waiter delivered the drinks.

Nathan had a rugged handsomeness to him. It was obvious he put in long hours of labour-intensive work daily. Shaggy brown hair and stubble that had grown into a short beard since she met him. He had rich brown eyes that never stopped looking at her. A delicious tan matched her own. He embodied everything that attracted her.

"I hope it's okay, I ordered beer and an appetizer."

"It is." He picked up the bottle and took a pull. "Did you have another bad day?"

"Do you think that's why I called you?"

"I'm glad you did, whatever the reason." Nathan leaned back while the waiter set the potato skins she ordered in the middle of the table, then took their orders.

"I called because I wanted to. It was a long day, but not a bad one."

"Have you heard from your friends since their revelation?"

Shaye shook her head. "And I'm not ready to reach out to them. I will, eventually. But their worries didn't go away just because I told them to leave me alone and I will not let them hover." She picked up a potato skin and dipped it in the sour cream. Nathan took a couple, but left the rest for her. By the time they emptied the plate, the waiter returned with the burgers.

"So, this is the burger you deem the best in town."

"It is," she said proudly. "And I'm right."

He laughed, the motion transforming his rough face. Shaye took a big bite and closed her eyes, moaning from the taste. She made a big show of how good the burger was. But when she opened her eyes, Nathan's burned with heat across from her. The sudden desire and arousal hit her in the chest.

When she called him, she hadn't been sure of her own intentions, if she planned to sleep with him again or not, but now, stopping herself seemed impossible. She looked away and took a drink of her beer, hoping it would cool her down.

"How's the bear?" Shaye blurted in the hopes to change the subject.

"He's fine." Mirth flirted around his mouth.

"You've seen him?"

Nathan paused, but nodded.

"What can you tell me about him?"

"I can't say much here."

Shaye frowned, her heart filling with uncertainty with his cryptic words.

"Come back to my place. There's something I want to tell you."

"Okay." She already knew she would end up in his bed again and she was eager to learn what he had to say. They finished their burgers and Nathan paid. She wondered if he would argue if she tried to pay. She was the one to invite him out, but it wasn't something she cared about. And it seemed, neither did he.

His hand on her back leading her out of the pub sent heated sparks through her body. They stopped next to their trucks, his parked beside hers.

"Do you want to bring your own truck or drop it off at home?" The question felt like it needed consideration. She'd be relying on him to leave his place.

"It's possible I'll need to work tomorrow. It might be the weekend, but I'm always on call."

"I can drive you if you need to go." It was a kind gesture, but Shaye narrowed her eyes, sensing something he wasn't saying.

"Are you offering out of consideration or do you have a reason for me not to have my truck?"

"You're too smart for your own good." He looked amused, but after a moment, he sobered and Shaye saw her instincts had been right.

"I have a reason."

Shaye laughed, looking at him with wide eyes and raised brows. "You know how that sounds, right?"

"I do." Despite her laughter, his eyes filled with so much sincerity.

"All right," she said, her voice softening. "Follow me home." They each walked to their trucks and Shaye spoke to herself under her breath. "I should worry about myself. This is delusional."

"No, you shouldn't. And you're not delusional," called Nathan from the other side of his truck. Shaye spun around, open-mouthed. How the hell did he hear her? He hopped in his truck and waited for her to do the same.

Shaye pulled away from Jackie's and watched Nathan's truck from her rear-view mirror. What reason would he have for her to depend on him for a ride? And why the hell would she agree to it?

The bear. He implied she could trust Nathan. She laughed to herself, the sound sudden in the cab of her truck. Of course she was delusional. She put her trust in a grizzly bear and some wild man that lived by the lake.

She parked her truck and took a steadying breath before getting out and joining Nathan in his. With locked eyes she said without words she was ready for whatever he had planned. She started this, and she would see it through.

THE RIDE WAS silent with tension filling the cab of his truck. Nathan's nerves couldn't douse the attraction between them that developed into a physical entity of its own. He was about to reveal himself to Shaye. He wasn't ready for it, but he didn't have a choice.

Nathan parked and met her on her side of the truck. Hoping to put it off, he kissed her. He wrapped her hair around his fist and kissed her until she melted against him. His other hand settled on her hip and moved to her ass as he slid his tongue along hers.

Their bodies lit on fire. His cock hardened and he smelled the moisture between her legs. His feet moved of their own accord and he started walking them back to the house. Guilt bubbled up, but it didn't register through the need to take her. Was he enough of an asshole to take advantage of this bond one more time, just to give him time before he had to tell her the truth?

With reluctance, he pulled his mouth away and stopped their progress. "Fuck."

"What is it?" Her husky voice did nothing to help him.

"I brought you here to tell you something. I should do that first."

"Uh, it can wait." Her brows twitched together.

Looking down at her, he threw a little mischief at her. "Eager to have your way with me?"

"I don't care who has their way with who, but we're going in that house." Her fingers flexed on his chest. He doubted she even noticed. And he pulled her closer so his cock rested against her belly.

"A demanding little bundle, aren't you?"

"Don't forget it," she whispered right before his lips met hers again. Maybe he shouldn't have kissed her to begin with, but at least he gave her the choice.

He moved his hands to lift her up the steps and set her down by the door to open it. As soon as they were through, he began working on her clothes. Her shirt over her head, her bra, her skirt and panties. Once she was bare in front of him, he stepped back. Dark pink nipples on rounded breasts, faint tan lines, tiny muscles on a small frame. She was amazing.

Shaye suddenly couldn't keep still, so he moved his eyes back to her face.

"You were looking at me so closely." Nathan hadn't associated her with being shy.

"I can look a lot closer." Her cheeks flamed and Nathan grinned, knowing he looked a little wicked. Her hair was askew from his grip. A few blonde strands escaped. He'd fix it soon. For now, he started working on his own clothes while he let his eyes roam over her body again. He pulled his shirt off. "Touch yourself for me, sweetness."

Her gasp was quick and sharp. Her hand inched from her side and slid over her hip and lower. She tentatively laid her finger over her clit. Nathan paused, watching until she moved her finger up and down. His cock strained painfully at his jeans. He undid the fly and pulled himself free for release.

Nathan didn't need to look up to know her eyes searched all over his body and now centred on his cock. They left a heat trail over his skin. He pulled his pants down and kicked them to the side.

He took himself in hand and stroked, matching her slow pace. His hand moved from base to tip, squeezing at the top before moving down. Nathan stepped backward and she took one forward. Her finger moved a little faster and so did his hand. Another step and she did too.

"That's right. Follow me." By the time they reached his bedroom door, both of them were panting. His orgasm built and he had to let go of his cock. He crooked his finger at Shaye for her to come the rest of the way to him. Her steps quickened, and she landed hard against his chest, her hands reaching up over his shoulders.

Nathan couldn't deny her anything. He bent his head and claimed her mouth. He prepared to lift her to throw her on the bed, but she pulled from the kiss and dropped to her knees.

"Jesus Christ, Shaye." She wrapped her hand around the base of his cock and guided the tip to her mouth. Her lips slid over him, the sight driving him insane. She slid her tongue over the sensitive head before pushing herself forward, engulfing him until he hit the back of her throat. He was already close before she started, but now he tried to hold it back. As much as he wanted to spill down her throat, right now he wanted the heat of her cunt. He wanted to mark her, but couldn't when she was on her knees in front of him. The best place for her to be.

To distract himself, he delved his fingers into her hair and took out the clip that still tried to hold half of it up. He ran his fingers through the blonde strands while her head bobbed back and forth and her tongue worked over the tip each time she reached it. Her light sucks drove him wild. He had no power left.

He gripped her hair and held her in place. Her eyes

darted upward to meet his. He thrust forcefully once, twice, then pulled out.

"I need to be inside your cunt. I promise to finish down your throat soon, but not right now." He pulled her from her knees and right off the floor. He tossed her on the bed and followed her down. Nathan had enough forethought to probe her entrance to make sure she was ready for him. He hadn't needed to worry. Her wetness coated his fingers. Guiding his cock, he lined himself up then grabbed her hip. "Hold on. This is going to be rough."

He thrust in, her heat encasing the length of him. She cried out and he groaned. Finally, he'd heard a sound from her pleasure. He intended to make her do it again. He pulled out and slammed home. Her cry turned into a moan, but was delicious all the same.

"Let me hear it all, sweetness." Their breath mingled between them. Nathan's teeth sharpened. Fuck, if he didn't move away from her throat he would mark her.

He slipped a hand between them to work on her clit. Her walls tightened around him and he groaned. Bending his head, he took a nipple into his mouth and sucked hard. Her back bowed, and her heat contracted, squeezing his cock. Light cries escaped her as she came.

The urge to bite her was too strong. He released her nipple and pulled out of her heat. With a tight grip on her hips, he flipped her over. He thrust in from behind, drinking in her scream as a new orgasm shuddered through her. It was enough to pull him over. He kept himself upright and pulled her hips back against him. He growled as he spilled deep inside her, and frustration took the place of satisfaction. Not marking her created a loss he didn't expect.

He collapsed to the bed and pulled her in his arms. Both of them were still trying to catch their breath. His body raged at him to do it again, to mark her, make her his. His cock never softened.

"Now, it's time to talk," he said between pants. He needed to tell her now before he lost what little control he had and took her again.

CHAPTER 8

Shaye had barely recovered from her orgasms and Nathan had returned from getting their clothes.

"We have to get out of bed to talk?" She rolled to her side and pulled on the pillow, exhaustion sinking her into the softness.

"Yeah, we do." His face was hard, and something about him seemed nervous. He held himself rigid beside the bed.

Shaye slowly stood and got dressed. Nathan put on his jeans. He took her hand and led her to the front door.

"We're going for a walk. You'll want your shoes." She frowned when he remained in his bare feet and no shirt. She raised a brow in question. "I don't need any." His broad frame towered over her and he looked down at her with unreadable, calm eyes.

"This isn't strange. Not at all." She tried to say as if it were true, but her sarcasm still made it through. Shaye saw a ghost of a smile play on his lip as he opened the door.

"The lake will have more light from the moon." They started hiking through the woods.

"What we need to talk about needs light?"

"We don't just need to talk. I need to show you something." He kept a tight hold on her hand and kept his eyes forward. Whatever he had to show her was important to him. Shaye still had pleasure humming through her veins, so it was easy for her to keep quiet until they reached the grassy bank by the lake.

But as they stopped, Nathan's body tensed. She watched the muscles in his arms and shoulders twitch and tighten. An unease crept over the back of her neck.

"What's going on, Nathan?" She set her hand on his arm.

"It's about your bear."

"*The* bear." She corrected. But she worried with the thought of something happening to him.

"He very much thinks of himself as your bear."

"How would you know?" She frowned.

Nathan sighed. "You said you didn't really believe in Fate."

"If Fate is real, she's a bitch." Shaye cursed every Deity out there for taking both her parents from her.

"Yeah, she can be."

"You believe in Fate?" He was the last person Shaye would have imagined believing in something like that.

"I have no choice. I have proof." He paused. "There's more than just Fate out there."

"Nathan, it will be easier if you just skip the explanation and tell me. Then you can explain it."

He nodded. "I'm the bear."

"Huh?" She must have misunderstood what he said.

Nathan stepped back and unbuttoned his jeans.

"What are you doing?"

"Showing you."

He took two more steps back and something happened. She heard bones popping and parts of Nathan's body moved out of place. Shaye put her hands to her mouth and watched in shock. His body and face changed shape and brown fur grew. At the point that his hands turned into paws, he hit the ground, brown swirls of air emanating from within him. It circled him to finish the change and settled back inside.

Rich brown eyes of the bear she first met by the lake stared at her.

"You're the bear." Her voice was breathy. "That's not possible."

Cautiously, he stepped forward. Shaye's instincts told her to step back. She moved a foot behind her, but stopped and moved it back into place. When he reached her, he made all the same motions he did the last time she saw him. He nuzzled her belly and her chest. He moved down to nuzzle between her legs, which she now understood why. After inhaling, he pushed his head under her hand.

"Nathan?" The bear nodded his head. "So you could answer me." He nodded again. She ran her hands through his fur and watched his eyes close. "This is amazing. But how?"

Nathan stepped back. Shaye watched the change happen, but this time in reverse. The brown air swirled around him until he took the shape of a human again. She winced when she heard bones popping as everything moved back into place.

"It doesn't hurt that much," he said, his voice rough from the change. She stared at him. "I'm a shifter."

"How?"

"That's a bit of a story, but the short version is I met a bear and her cub when I was little. I don't remember much except a brown wind that circled myself and the cub. That was the first night I changed."

"How old were you?"

"Four." He reached for his pants and pulled them on.

"Wow. There's so much to process."

"There's more." Nathan stepped closer and took her hands. "Something I learned recently about shifters is that we have mates. Mates aren't chosen by us."

"You are not about to say what I think you're about to say." She shook her head, denial bubbling up fast and fierce.

"I am. I found you here by the lake for the first time because something drew me to you. The brown wind I mentioned? It was trying to get me to find you the first night you arrived. I fought it off for a little while. The result was an uncontrolled shift, and my animal instincts took over to search for you."

"How did you find me?"

"Your scent. It's how I recognized you as my mate. It's unique, strong. It made me weak and dizzy until I approached you."

"Do I have a say in any of this?"

"You tell me. Can you walk away from me? Do you want to walk away?"

"I don't know. But it's tempting to try. To prove a point." Shaye recognized her father's stubbornness in her tone. Nathan smiled, but sobered quickly.

"There's one more thing I need to tell you."

"Of course there is." Her arms floated down to her sides.

"Shifters mark their mates."

"That sounds bad."

"I almost marked you back at the house. I don't know how I stopped myself. There's an emptiness in my chest from the loss of it."

"You wanted to tell me first," she said, softening with his consideration.

"You deserve that much. I didn't know about mates only

a few months ago. If I'd met you before then, I wouldn't have had enough control to stop myself." He tucked her hair behind her ear. "I might not be able to stop it next time."

Flutters begin low in Shaye's belly and her core throbbed. Her breath turned short, and she craved for his touch. "I can feel it. This isn't fair."

"I won't disagree with you. I didn't want to find a mate. You're getting the shit end of this deal." He leaned forward, their foreheads touching.

Shaye tried to focus through the haze of desire clouding her mind. "What do you mean?"

"No one deserves what I bring to a relationship." When she had braced herself to pull away from him, from Fate's decisions, he had to say something like that. Fate was an asshole. Shaye wanted a choice in this. She wanted to know if she could choose Nathan on her own, not because it was meant to be. But she couldn't walk away from him now. And if she didn't, he would mark her, which she assumed sealed them together.

"Damn it, Nathan." She pushed him away. "I want to go."

"I'll take you home." His words sounded like they rolled over gravel.

She was hurting him. And she had the same pain growing in her chest. They kept their distance while they walked back to the truck.

He let her in, while he went inside to get the keys.

The air was thick, frustration and desire mixed. He parked behind her truck, then reached over to pick up her hand. He kissed her wrist. Heat seared up her arm. She wanted to say something, but if she did, it would be to tell him to turn around and take her back. She couldn't risk letting anything out.

He released her, and she slowly got out of the truck and

walked to her door. She squeezed her eyes shut to keep herself from looking back at him. She wanted the choice. It had to be her choice to go to him. Fate already chose who was or wasn't in her life. She wouldn't choose this too.

"I NEED A FAVOUR." Nathan rolled his shoulders as he talked into his phone to Asher. Fuck, he hated asking him for anything, but it was the middle of the night, and he already knew he wouldn't be capable in the morning.

"Anything." Asher's groggy voice sharpened.

"Call the lumber yard for me in the morning. Make whatever excuse you need to." His bones popped and his voice changed.

"You got it." Asher's easy acceptance floored Nathan. Nathan hadn't given the guy much. He showed up, but he was standoffish, sometimes rude. And yet Asher was still there for him, all because he was a shifter too and understood. Nathan needed to do better for them.

Asher was about to say more, but Nathan hung up. He didn't have time to explain. He shucked his jeans and made it back outside in time for his body to change and grow.

He roared into the night. Desperation clawed at him. He didn't know if he'd just lost his mate, but his insides were in pain as if he did. She pulled back. She asked to leave. Nathan was proud of her strength. But that didn't ease his agony.

Bear walked around from the side of his house.

She'll be back, he said confidently, already knowing his problem as a brother should.

I hope you're right.

Nathan followed Bear deeper into the woods, back to

their den where they grew up. He spent so many years as a bear before ever dealing with his mother's death and the little shack they lived in. Auntie, Bear's mother, helped him bury his mother, but he never shifted back to a little boy. She got rid of the bodies of the men first. Somehow, she understood what Nathan needed and what he needed to do.

That house had remained abandoned. They'd spotted people searching the place for his mother and him when she hadn't shown up for work. As he got older, he'd assumed they had searched for them both, however it was obvious his mother was gone. Nathan never remembered her name on his own. It wasn't until he was much older he went back to the house. He'd lived in it alone for a while when he tried to attend school. Without parents to register him, he'd had to sneak into classes to learn. Sometimes he'd get caught in the first class. Other times he had got a few weeks in before they realized he wasn't supposed to be there. It had been easier to do in high school classes. When he couldn't get into schools, he'd used the library, spending hours hidden in the corners absorbing everything he could.

The hardest part was making sure he had looked like he belonged. He'd been careful when raiding charity bins for clothes. He remembered his first time. Auntie had convinced him he needed to shift back and deal with the other half of his life. He hadn't wanted to. Life was easier as a bear. But she'd finally made him do it. In the middle of the night, she stood by him while he shifted. It had been rough. He didn't really know how. He'd been asleep when he first shifted to a bear cub the night they killed his mother. The more frustrated he got, the more difficult it had become. By the end, he had been on the ground in tears.

She walked him into town and they had found a bin of clothes. He'd rifled through it, trying several on and taking anything else that would fit him. Then she took him home. Not to the den, to the house.

Nathan suddenly realized he was growling, a consistent rumble in his chest, pulling him away from his memories. His life was a fucking mess. And Fate wanted to force Shaye to have him, the fucking bitch. Shaye didn't deserve this. Her life had enough heartache she didn't need to be saddled with someone with his history.

The two grizzlies settled in the den, but Nathan never slept. Eventually, Bear lifted his head.

Come on. Let's try to sleep by the lake.

No. I can't go to the lake. He couldn't sit there and not think about Shaye. Her name alone through his mind had pain tearing his insides.

Too bad. We're going.

Nathan growled. When Bear growled back, Nathan stood, ready for a fight.

This is what you want instead. Fine, brother. Bear backed out of the den and dug in his claws. Nathan charged and ran into him head on. Bear braced himself and pushed back. Nathan wasn't fighting smart, and he didn't care. Deep down he knew Bear would beat him, but maybe after a fight Nathan would feel better.

Bear stood on his hind legs and came down on Nathan's head before he pushed himself upright. Nathan shook his head and dodged his next attack, getting himself back on his feet. They met in the air, claws slashing forward. As they came down, Bear sank his teeth into Nathan's shoulder. He roared through the pain until Bear let go.

Panting, Nathan stared at Bear.

Done? Bear asked.

Nathan didn't answer. He charged.

Bear's paw was in the air before Nathan saw his mistake.

The impact swung his head to the side, pain setting stars in his vision. That's when Nathan gave up. Fighting with Bear wouldn't bring Shaye back or fix the pain of being away from her.

We're going to the lake. Bear's authority mirrored Auntie's, his mother's. Auntie had been a force all on her own. She'd protected both of them as they grew slower than all the other cubs. Slower growth, longer life. For Bear anyway. His growth matched Nathan's so he would always be by his side, his brother.

Nathan slowly pushed himself back up and followed Bear, defeat bearing down on him. Not from losing to Bear. From losing the life he could have had and from losing his mate before he ever had her.

Shaye washed her face and brushed her teeth for the third time since Nathan dropped her off the night before. She was late for work, but there was no way she was calling in sick over this. Her misery began the moment she pushed Nathan away. As it grew, it turned to nausea.

She showered and got dressed, ready to walk out the door, but her stomach turned over another time. She gripped her abdomen and swallowed down. Standing in her living room, she let a scream erupt from her lungs.

"No! You will not do this to me!" Shaye screamed into the emptiness of her home. "You've taken my family from me. I refuse to let you decide my life."

A few slow breaths in and the nausea passed. If possible, the room felt emptier than before. The ache in her chest never went away, but at least she wouldn't be sick again.

She made it to work, although her movements were unsteady.

"Shaye? Are you all right?" Her boss, Diana, might be demanding, but at least she cared.

"I'm fine. I'm sorry I'm late." She set her bag down on her desk and booted her computer.

"You are not fine. You look awful." Diana put her hands on her hips. "Are you sure you should be here?"

"I'm sure. I'm not sick." Shaye said it not only to Diana, but to whoever, or whatever, was listening. And to herself.

"Okay." She nodded. "We have three viewings this morning. You have time to get through the messages and such first, but then we need to hurry."

Shaye had to push herself to get through it all, but she didn't do the best she could. She was much more pleasant when handling clients, but today she did the bare minimum without appearing rude.

Eventually, Diana got pissed off enough she sent Shaye home. "There's something wrong with you today. Since you insist you aren't sick, then you need to go home and fix whatever your problem is. I need you back here as your normal self tomorrow."

Shaye sat in her truck in her driveway, not knowing where to go or what to do. She didn't want to go inside, and she refused to go to Nathan. Yet.

"Please." Shaye begged. "Just let me decide for myself. How do you know I wouldn't choose him without your interference?"

She stopped fighting and cried. With her only other option to return to Nathan, maybe letting out her tears would allow the pain to escape.

It wasn't as if she'd never grieved for her father, or her

mother once she'd been old enough to understand, but she shed fresh tears for each of them now.

Wiping at her eyes and sniffling, she tried to stop the flow. It felt good to let it out, but crying hadn't been what she needed right now. She tried to eat something. Even with her weak appetite, the sandwich stayed down. Her body heaved with exhaustion. She took a shower and lay down in bed. Her sleep wasn't sound, and her throbbing chest acted like a weight to keep her down.

Her boss told her to fix this. How could she fix this? All she wanted to know was if she would choose Nathan on her own, not because Fate planned her life that way. It wasn't only Nathan she had to choose. He was something magical. She needed to prepare for whatever life that brought her. She hadn't stuck around long enough to discover what that life entailed.

CHAPTER 9

Nathan got lost in the animal. He wandered the woods and the lake with Bear while the pain burrowed and created a home. It didn't leave him, it never would, but it receded enough he was no longer angry. Night was falling again, and Nathan made his way home. He tried to shift, but it hurt. He couldn't finish and reverted back to his animal form.

His phone rang inside the house. It didn't matter. He lay on the ground and waited for whatever came next.

A truck pulled up. He recognized the sound, but it wasn't the one he hoped for. Soon, the smell of a wolf grew stronger. The truck shut off and he heard the door shut. Nathan let the wolf get his bearings before he walked around the house. There was no point pretending he wasn't there. Asher would smell him.

"I take it this means you need me to make excuses again tomorrow? They won't buy anything for long from someone they don't know. They will want to talk to you."

Nathan bobbed his head.

"What's happened?"

He hung his head and turned away. He didn't want or need company. Nathan sighed at the sound of bones popping and the rush of a warm breeze. When he turned around, a large white wolf stood in place of Asher.

What happened? I only want to help.

You can't. Even inside his head, Nathan sounded savage. His nerves felt harsh, his anger rough against them.

Is it your mate?

Nathan growled low. *This isn't any of your business.*

The wolf lifted his nose into the air. *She isn't here.*

Want a gold star, detective?

Nathan, you need to go find her.

There's a problem with that. She doesn't want interference. She's pissed off at being forced together. Nathan shook his head. *Go away, Asher.*

You need to give her reasons she would choose you herself.

You don't know what you're talking about, Dr. Wolf. Fuck off. He wouldn't listen to the privileged alpha.

Asher growled, his teeth showing, and the fur behind his neck stood on end. Aggression met with aggression. Nathan showed his teeth and braced his paws. Just as they charged, Shaye's truck pulled up and parked beside Asher's. Her headlights shined bright on both shifters. Nathan and Asher collided, jaws gnashing and paws pushing.

The truck horn blared, once, twice, but the shifters ignored it. Shaye must have held her hand down on her steering wheel because the horn never stopped. Asher and Nathan winced and pulled back. The sound echoed in Nathan's ears. He shook his head and Asher swatted an ear before he glared back at Nathan.

Is that her? She smells like you. Asher already had his answer. Nathan remained silent.

Shaye got out of her truck. "Nathan?" She left her door open and took a cautious step around it.

Something eased inside him. His mate was here, but it might not be enough.

Asher was swinging his head back and forth, looking between Nathan and Shaye. *You going to talk to her?*

I can't shift.

What do you mean you can't shift? Asher faced him, giving his back to Shaye. Nathan watched her grab her door and brace herself to run.

I tried before you got here. I can't shift.

Asher nodded, although it was obvious he didn't understand. He walked over to his pile of clothes and picked up his jeans. Behind his truck, he shifted, the swirl of white appearing for a moment above the hood. Asher stood again as a man and pulled on his jeans before coming back out to meet Shaye.

"Hi. I'm Asher Morestead." He held out his hand. Nathan saw the hesitation in Shaye's eyes, but she shook his hand.

"You're a wolf."

"I am." Asher smiled gently. "And you are?"

"Shaye. Tierney."

"It's nice to meet you, Shaye."

"Um, you too. I need to talk to Nathan."

"Nathan can't..."

Nathan growled, cutting Asher off. The last thing he wanted Shaye to know was that he was having trouble shifting. Asher reared back, his brows raised at Nathan.

"Never mind."

"No. Not never mind." She pointed her finger at Nathan. "If there's something I should know, then one of you will tell me."

Asher was watching him, waiting to see how he wanted

to handle this. Nathan was thankful for that. He didn't give the privileged veterinarian enough credit.

Nathan closed his eyes and attempted to shift. His bones popped, but pain seared through him and parts refused to move. The magic from within tried to take over, but there wasn't enough. He reverted. Nathan sighed and nodded at Asher.

"He can't shift," Asher said to Shaye.

"Why?"

"I'm not sure."

"I guess I'll be able to talk, and he can listen." She was attempting a joke, but her tone said otherwise. A fresh pain started low in his gut. He suspected she would attempt to end this permanently. Asher looked nervously between the two of them.

"Shaye, has he explained everything?"

"How would I know?"

Asher hedged. "Has he explained about the two of you?"

"That Fate chose me as his mate? Yeah, he mentioned that." Bitterness laced her voice, and he couldn't blame her for it. He felt the same.

"We don't know many shifters and therefore don't know many with mates. In fact, he and I are the only ones. My mate's name is Gwen. She would be more than willing to help you with anything you need. Even if all you have is questions."

Shaye frowned and looked away in the direction of the lake. After a few minutes, she met Nathan's eyes. She didn't look back at Asher when she answered. "I think I'd like that." She sighed. "But I'd like to talk to Nathan first. Do you mind waiting a few minutes so I can follow you back?"

"Of course."

Nathan gave a short growl to get Asher's attention and he nodded toward his back.

"I think Nathan is offering you a ride to my place."

"How?"

Asher's lips twitched. "On his back."

"Maybe." Her voice faded. She walked toward the lake and left Nathan to catch up.

His mate was back, but it wasn't necessarily a good thing. Although if she is willing to talk to Gwen, then she wasn't pushing him away yet. His gut turned with fear of what she was about to say.

She sat on the bank and looked at him, questions showing in her eyes while he lay down beside her. He should have kept some distance, but he didn't. He laid his head in her lap. His eyes closed as she ran her fingers through his fur.

"I've been sick since you dropped me off last night. I stood in my living room to scream at Fate, telling her to fuck off. And I did it again sitting alone in my truck. Then I begged her to fuck off. She hasn't. But I can think a little now. Would I choose you? If you weren't a shifter. If Fate didn't exist. If there wasn't such a thing as a mate. Would I still choose you? Then, would I choose this life? I don't know what this life is like. Maybe I left too soon yesterday, but if I had stayed, things would have moved to a step we couldn't take back. And maybe I'm putting both of us through unnecessary pain and all of this thinking and wondering and choosing for myself is for nothing. Fate will win in the end, because that's what She does. Is the reason you can't shift because I left?"

There wasn't a straightforward answer to that, but he couldn't leave it unanswered, so he nodded once then shook his head.

"I'll take that as a yes and a no. I'm sorry." He nuzzled her belly, hoping she understood he wasn't upset with her. "I think talking to Asher's mate is a good idea. I promise I'll be back. I know you want to take me, but you should stay here if you're having trouble."

Nathan stood and stepped back. Again, he tried to shift, but all he ended with was a burning sensation through his limbs. He growled and swung his head. Shaye appeared in front of him. She wrapped her arms around his neck.

"I'll be back tonight. I promise."

Nathan didn't have any intentions of staying here to wait for her, but he had no way to tell her that. Where she went, so did he.

SHAYE LEFT Nathan at the lake. Tears slid down her cheeks in silent drops. He couldn't shift. What if she couldn't stay with him? What would happen? She hoped Gwen had the answers she needed. She dried her cheeks before she was in sight of Asher leaning against his red truck. At least he had dressed. Not that he was awful to look at, but she wasn't interested.

"Still want to follow?" He pushed off his truck.

"Yes, please." She hopped into her own and backed out of his way so he could precede her. Asher lived on the opposite side of town, down a gravel road leading into the woods. Shifters seemed to like their wilderness. She smirked. Her kind of people.

Asher led her inside the house, and a short brunette met them at the door.

"I thought I heard an unfamiliar truck." She was about

an inch shorter than Shaye. Freckles danced on her face when she smiled.

"Shaye, this is Gwen. This is Nathan's mate, Shaye Tierney."

"Nathan's mate? Nathan? That Nathan?"

Shaye took a step back. Why would it be so surprising for Nathan to have a mate? There had to be more she didn't understand.

"Gwen." Asher laid a hand on her shoulder. "Yes, that Nathan, but calm down. You're making her nervous."

"Oh, my God. I'm sorry. I'm just shocked."

"I couldn't tell," she replied dryly. Gwen's face split into a wide smile.

"I like you." She thrust the dish towel she was holding into Asher's chest. "You can finish cleaning." She took one step toward Shaye, but Asher's hand came out to stop her by curving around the base of her throat. Gwen leaned her head back and looked up at him. His eyes flashed a brilliant blue.

"Yes, Ma'am." He kissed her, slow and sweet, then released her. Gwen's cheeks brightened to a light pink as she grabbed Shaye's hand and pulled them both outside to sit in the wooden Adirondack chairs on the porch.

"How did you know this is what I wanted?" Shaye asked.

Gwen shrugged. "I assumed."

"I have questions." Shaye turned her locket over and back.

"I'm not sure how much help I can be. Not that long ago I went through this, so I'm still learning too."

"How did you handle Fate forcing the choice on you?"

"Woah, you don't start small. Well, pretty good. I had other issues than just a mate bond to deal with."

"Other issues?"

"Psychotic friend and a lone wolf. Nothing related to being a mate. I'll tell you all of that another time."

"It didn't bother you that Fate made your choice for you?"

Gwen's lips twisted to the side, and she looked off in the distance. "The thought crossed my mind, but I didn't fight it. I believed I would have chosen Asher on my own."

"Did you ever try to figure out if you would have chosen him without Fate's interference?"

"No. Who's to say Fate doesn't have something to do with all our choices? Our careers. Our friends. Which route we take to work every day. Or the reason we choose a different road, or a different coffee shop from our daily routines."

Shaye had to suck in a breath and grit her teeth. Gwen's words reflected so much of Shaye's life.

"Are you okay?"

"Yeah." Shaye's enthusiasm gave her away. "Yeah, I'm fine."

"Something I tracked after Asher first sealed the mate bond was the effect it had on me. He didn't know any other shifters, let alone other mates. Neither of us had any idea what would happen. But what did happen was an increase to my own senses. They don't reach the strength of a shifter, but I have an increased sense of smell and hearing. And with those, I'm learning to detect emotions. Asher's been helping me learn to distinguish between them. But at this point, I can tell when something is wrong."

"Mate's change... wait," Shaye frowned, "what do you mean sealed the mate bond? There's a bond that exists before the mark?"

"Don't you feel it? You must, or you wouldn't be here." Gwen turned in the oversized chair to sit sideways and criss-crossed her legs.

Shaye had to close her eyes. She felt it. That was what made her so sick when she left and tried to fight it. That was what kept him on her mind. "Do you believe Fate controls that much? All the tiny details of our lives?"

"Maybe it is only the tiny details she controls."

Shaye looked up. "What do you mean?"

"The tiny details are small pieces to a large puzzle. She helps put them in place. Part of me believes she's only helping a different magic out there."

"So, I'm overthinking all of this." Shaye put her face in her hands. She was causing them both awful pain.

"No. I don't think so. It's okay for you to not want to be controlled. I loved Asher, whether or not Fate was involved. My choice aligned with Fate's."

"That's my problem. I don't know what my choice would be."

"You do." Gwen nodded confidently. "Deep down you do. Or this wouldn't be meant to be. Would you be forced together only to be miserable?"

Shaye looked at Gwen, who held a soft smile. She was being an idiot. She laughed. The laugh grew until her belly shook and her lungs hurt, stealing her breath. Gwen was laughing too. "Could you imagine?" She squeaked between gasps.

"Growing old and still cursing each other." Gwen threw her head back. "I can see Nathan now."

"A grumpy old man in the woods." Shaye added.

They wiped the tears from their eyes as they calmed.

"You make it all sound simple."

"I learned that from Asher."

Shaye took in a steadying breath and looked across the lawn. A pair of brown eyes flashed from between the trees. "He followed me here."

"He's been here for at least ten minutes."

Shaye turned to the other woman. "Thank you." She hoped her sincerity was visible.

"Anytime. I mean that."

Shaye squeezed Gwen's hand and stood to walk toward the bear waiting for her.

NATHAN'S HEART pounded as he watched Shaye slowly walk across Asher's lawn. His skin crawled to shift so he could touch her, hold her, but he didn't dare try. She stepped into the trees and stopped in front of him.

"I can't stay away, Nathan. That much is clear. I'm still not happy about Fate poking her nose in my decisions, but Gwen gave me some things to think about. Can I think about those things while being with you?"

It was enough for Nathan, for now. He quickly closed the distance between them and ran his head over her chest and belly. His eyes closed with the pleasure her scent poured into him.

"But I have a request." Her voice softened. "Can you hold off on marking me for a little while longer?"

That was no small request. And Nathan didn't have an answer for her. It wasn't something he could promise. His control had been almost non-existent the last time they were together. Unless he stayed as a bear, he would mark her. He looked up at her, hoping everything he needed to say showed in his eyes.

"I guess I won't know what you're saying until you can shift again." She ran her hand over his head and down his neck. "You're magnificent. And so soft. And I'm so tired." Her hand dropped away. "Meet you at your place?"

Nathan bobbed his head and nuzzled her one last time. He walked out to her truck with her.

"How are you going to get back?"

Nathan tilted his head.

"Right, same way you got here, I'm sure." She got in her truck and turned it around to drive back down the lane.

When Nathan turned around, he saw Asher and Gwen standing together on their deck. He owed them both his gratitude. He bent his head low. Asher acknowledged it with his own nod, and Gwen waved. Once he shifted again, he would thank them properly. Asher really was creating what he said he would. They might be small potatoes now, but they would grow. And Nathan would be part of it.

He ran toward the trees and started for home. It took longer for him to get there than Shaye. Even being late at night and being able to cut through the quiet parts of town, he still had to travel as much through woods as possible.

Shaye sat on his front step when he walked toward her from the direction of the lake.

"Can you shift?"

Nathan had a decision. He could try to either feel the pain and stay a bear or it could work and he would be a man again. But as a man, he wouldn't be able to hold himself back from her. He searched her eyes. Guilt hovered in a faint cloud over the orbs. She blamed herself.

He closed his eyes and started the shift. Body parts moved and the ache spread through him, slowly increasing in its intensity. The change took too long and turned painful. He roared and let go, his body reverting. Nathan sagged to the ground.

"I'm so sorry." Shaye wrapped her arms around herself. Nathan shook his head. This wasn't her fault. The sheen in her eyes hurt to look at. He didn't want to see his mate hurting.

He pulled in his strength and lifted himself off the ground. A few steps and he could set his head in her lap. She leaned forward and wrapped herself around him. It was the contact they both needed. To know that she was in similar pain as him when they separated bothered him. If she left him out of spite for Fate, her life would be miserable. There was no right decision.

With a sigh, she lifted herself up. Not only did she look exhausted, she felt it too. He sensed the fatigue in her body. Nathan pushed her with his nose, nudging until she stood. He nodded to the door.

"Yeah, I'm going." With one last pet, she went inside.

Nathan closed his eyes and collapsed to the ground. He needed just as much rest as Shaye. And now that she was near, he could. What he wouldn't do is condemn Shaye to life with him if it wasn't what she wanted.

CHAPTER 10

All too soon, Shaye's alarm on her phone chimed. It didn't matter how she still felt on the inside. Diana needed her at work. Swiping the screen to shut it off, she set her phone beside her and rubbed at her eyes. Her heavy and swollen lids would need a lot of caffeine to open for the day. She hoped the pain and nausea had gone. She wouldn't be able to work through those again.

Pushing herself up, she swung her legs over the side of Nathan's bed. All she needed was the smell of him on his sheets the night before to put her into a deep sleep. Even if it was only for a few hours. She did a mental check on herself before pushing herself up onto her feet. Her head ached a little, but there weren't anymore body aches and her stomach had stopped churning. At least for now.

Shaye searched Nathan's house for a bathroom. After she finished, she splashed some water on her face and brushed her teeth with her finger. It was enough to get home to shower and change. Diana would notice if she showed up in the same clothes as yesterday. And she wouldn't be happy about it, assuming that if she noticed, then so would clients.

She eyed Nathan's kitchen. Maybe he had coffee. But searching and waiting for it to brew now would take more time than running her own machine or grabbing some on the way to work. She sighed, out of ways to procrastinate. Shaye opened the front door and stepped out. She expected to see a bear, but saw Nathan sleeping naked in the grass. He was face down, his arms over his head and one knee bent to the side. Even his backside was sculpted. Shaye wouldn't be the woman she was if she didn't take even a moment to appreciate that.

She took a step down and the creaking of the stair startled him. He bolted up, landing on his hands and knees. He looked down.

"Nathan. You shifted."

He pushed himself up and stood, his hand going to his head. "It must have happened while I slept."

A phone rang from inside the house. Nathan walked past her, his hand running across her midriff as he passed. Warmth spread through her body from his touch. Peace. A reconnection. How had she not seen this before?

She stepped back up to the door and listened.

"Yeah, I'm back. Thanks again." He hung up and turned to her.

"I need to go get ready for work. I can't miss another day."

"You didn't get in yesterday?" He walked over to her. He didn't touch her, but he was close enough she could see the morning dew that clung to his skin and the scent of it filled her senses.

"I did, but I had to leave early."

He lifted his hand and cupped her jaw. Shaye couldn't

stop herself from leaning her face against his hand. "Come back after work. Please."

"I will." She paused, knowing now wasn't the best time to ask. "Nathan, about my request." He closed his eyes and turned his head. When he looked back at her, his eyes had changed. They flashed and looked more like the shape of a bear's.

"I can't promise, but I will try."

"Thank you." She knew she should turn away then, but they both seemed frozen in the moment. Nathan moved first. He bent his head and kissed her. He claimed her mouth, reclaimed her. With gentle lips, he worked until she melted against him and he wrapped his arms around her. His cock hardened against her belly and she became blatantly aware this could turn into something more very quickly. The heat built between their bodies, flames licking up their abdomens to wrap around their shoulders.

Shaye inhaled, allowing his scent to seep into her body to hold throughout the day. With reluctance, he pulled back. He turned her around and gently urged her back outside. She walked on unsteady legs that shivered from a sudden chill to her truck. Before she pulled out, she lifted her hand to wave at a deliciously naked Nathan leaning in an open door.

Today would not be easy. Shower and coffee. Small steps. Small goals. That's how she planned to manage. And in between it all, she would imagine Nathan exactly how she left him.

NATHAN THREW himself in a cold shower. It was a cruel punishment, but he needed to regain some awareness to pull him back into reality. This was far from over. Shaye hadn't agreed to be his mate and Nathan wouldn't force her, but he feared the consequences for denying what was meant to be. They only had a taste of the pain they could be in. If he'd marked her and they separated, the pain would be unbearable.

This life was a fucking curse. Or a blessing. It depended on the day.

He went into work, thankful they bought Asher's food poisoning tale. The day wasn't easy. His sorrow sat at the edges of his consciousness, waiting to take the place of the pain when Shaye left for good. He needed her, but he'd never tell her that.

Nathan called Shaye at lunch to ask what time she would finish and said he had an errand to run after work, but wouldn't be long. He left work early and drove to Asher's. He stepped up onto his deck and the door swung open before he knocked.

"Come on in." Asher held the door and Gwen stood behind him.

"I can't stay long. I came because I owe both of you my thanks. And an apology." He met Asher's eyes. "I haven't been very involved in what you're trying to create. You both came through and helped me with no explanation. Thank you. And it showed me the value in what you're doing."

"I think that's the most I've ever heard you say at one time," said Gwen, stepping forward beside her mate.

"It sure is." Asher agreed. "And you're welcome. This is why I'm doing this. We shouldn't be alone."

"Did Shaye decide to stay with you?" Gwen asked.

"For now." Nathan hesitated with what he wanted to offer next. He wasn't used to having people around, but it was the least he could do. "You know my home is well isolated on the opposite side of town. If anyone finds themselves in need of space or clothing, my place is safe."

"Thank you, Nathan." Asher held out his hand and Nathan shook it. It was a contribution.

Nathan left feeling a little lighter. He stopped to pick up pizza on the way home and pulled up to his place behind Shaye. They met in front of their trucks. His eyes flashed and her gasp registered. Nathan had to set the pizza box down on the hood of his truck or he would have dropped it with the way his hands itched. They wrapped around her waist and pulled her against him. It was impossible for him not to touch her. He bent his head and kissed her, working hard to keep it gentle. If he took it too far, they would lose control, and he promised her he'd try. Her body softened against his and he had to pull away.

He turned her away from him toward the house and grabbed the pizza. She pulled in a slow breath and took measured steps. Her face tilted over her shoulder, but her eyes were cast downward. Nathan followed her and they both made it inside without tripping over themselves.

He set the pizza down on the table and opened the box. "I hope this is okay."

"It's great." Shaye sat down and reached for a slice. He didn't bother with plates. They ate from the box, an awkward tension forming in the silence.

Shaye set her half-eaten slice back in the box and slowly brought her eyes up to meet his.

"Nathan. I need to know something. I need to know how you feel about Fate creating this and taking this choice from us." Shaye squared her shoulders and straightened her spine. Nathan looked at her resolute posture, feeling her determination and fear, and chose his words carefully. He stood to get beer from the fridge, buying himself a few minutes. He set the bottles on the table and turned his chair sideways before sitting down again. Leaning forward, he rested his elbows on his knees.

"I have a different answer to that depending on why I'm asking if I resent Fate. I can't say it hasn't been a blessing. But it's been a fucking curse, too. I can claim both for the situation She's put us in now."

Shaye's shoulder sagged, but she pulled herself back up. "Give me the bad first."

"You don't deserve to be forced to be with something like me. My past is ugly and there are parts of it even I don't know. I'm nothing special. I'm just a grumpy man living alone in the woods." Nathan let his lips twitch, but Shaye didn't follow his humour, using her own words from her conversation with Gwen. Her eyes found his and fierceness overtook her brow.

"Your past isn't who you are now." She shook her head. "And the good?"

"You." She was his blessing. He didn't deserve her, but Fate was trying to give her to him, anyway. Shaye licked her lips and adjusted herself in her seat.

"Do you resent Fate for making you a shifter?"

"I'm not sure it was all Fate's doing. But I have the same answer. A blessing and a fucking curse." He shut his eyes to block out the worst memory he held inside his mind. "I would have died the same night as my mother if I weren't meant to be a shifter. And if I weren't, and I had lived past that night, maybe I would have had a normal childhood and grown up with a family." On and off he'd imagined going to school while his mother worked. He'd imagined buying a new house, just him and his mom. Then maybe one day she would have found another man, another father for Nathan. He could have had brothers and sisters.

Nathan clenched his jaw and shut down the childish wishes.

Shaye's fingers hovered over her lips.

"There's one magical thing I trust and follow and I don't think it's Fate. That magic, the auburn wind, is what led me to you."

"Gwen gave me a new perspective, and it's one I'm struggling with."

Nathan reached up and gripped her chin. "I'm here." He leaned forward and sealed his vow with a kiss. Just tasting her was risking going too far. He pulled back and gritted his teeth. One more breath and he could speak. "Let's take a walk to the lake."

"Okay," she whispered. The lake was safe.

THE TIME at the lake was peaceful and exactly what Shaye needed. She smiled when Nathan handed her his fishing rod and tackle box before leaving. They barely knew each other, yet he knew this is what she enjoyed. A simple consideration that meant more to her than any words or promises. That he would think of this for her went a long way in helping to sort her thoughts. To see if this was a decision she would make, if he was who she would choose. Gwen's words made more sense than her anger and assumptions.

If Fate held the control Shaye believed, then free will didn't exist at all. But if all Fate did was place pieces of a puzzle together... Shaye sighed. She felt Nathan's eyes shift toward her while he walked beside her, but he said nothing. She was thankful. There wasn't anymore to say about this. She had to let it ride out.

But if he marked her, that would be it.

She sat at the edge of the bank and searched through Nathan's tackle box to see what lures he had. When she looked up, Nathan was pulling his shirt off over his head.

Shaye shamelessly took in the view of his wide shoulders and sculpted torso. His coarse chest hair matched the light brown on his head, but it hid nothing. She moved her eyes lower, following the thinning trail of hair down to that sexy V.

He cleared his throat and Shaye slowly lifted her eyes to his, but they didn't stay there long. She let them roam back down his body. His hands worked open the fly of his jeans. He wasn't wearing underwear. She supposed it was just another piece of clothing to worry about when shifting back and forth. His cock, rigid and long, sprang free. Shaye sucked her bottom lip between her teeth.

"Jesus fucking Christ, Shaye." He cursed low. She looked up at his face and saw he had his eyes squeezed shut. His body began to move and pop, parts moving in ways they shouldn't. Painful magic. When the brown swirls finally lifted, a bear stood in his place. Her bear.

Damn it. He was her bear. She already knew that. She decided to go back to the lake to meet him while camping with her friends. She decided to come back alone, not once, but twice. Camping at this lake wasn't new for her, and she'd been making her way around this lake for years. Fate's puzzle pieces. Her stepping stones.

She suddenly felt raw and exposed. Her fight had been a barrier to what she was really feeling. She still didn't like Fate meddling in her life. She was the one that created the pieces that took her parents from her. But Nathan was right. There were two sides.

Shaye made herself busy with the tackle box, choosing

what she needed. She set the hook. Pulling the rod back, she looked over her shoulder as she cast it forward and let go of the reel. The hook sank into the water with a plop.

Nathan walked over and nuzzled her neck, brushing her hair back. Then his heavy gait took him toward the water. She watched him wade in while she slowly and gently reeled in to recast. He dunked himself in the water a few times, hung his head low and looked back and forth.

Shaye hooted with laughter when his head popped up with a fish flapping back and forth in his jaw. He turned his head to look at her and almost lost the fish. Quickly biting down again, he caught it, but lower on its tail. The front of the fish swung, hitting him in the eye. Shaye fell back on the ground, holding her stomach with one hand while her other still held the rod. She knew he wasn't impressed with the hilarious situation which had her laughing all the more.

She sat herself back up to concentrate on her own fishing. Nathan dropped the fish and stepped out of the water. She eyed him as he came closer. A few feet away, he paused, his eyes boring into her. Then he shook. Shaye screamed as water droplets flew from his fur and rained down on her. When he finished, he huffed out his nose and went back to the water. She started laughing all over again.

CHAPTER 11

Nathan didn't shift back until he heard Shaye in the shower. She'd set his clothes on the step before going inside. He took a deep breath before beginning the change. He feared shifting at the lake, but it was safer when Shaye was around. With his mate by his side, he should be able to shift freely, but a moment of concern he might be stuck again passed. He ignored it and focused his thoughts on Shaye.

The change began, and the sensation was a familiar one before the warmth of the magic spread and finished the job. He dressed and went inside. He pulled some spare blankets and pillows from the closet and made a bed for himself on the couch. He was sitting on the couch with a beer when she emerged from his room, her hair damp and askew and his t-shirt hanging to her knees.

His nostrils flared taking in the scent of his body wash attempting to cover her natural scent. It couldn't be hidden from him.

She halted when she saw the blanket and pillow on the couch. "Oh." She looked hurt.

"It's for me, sweetness."

"Do you have to?" An innocent hope lingered in her voice.

"Yeah. If you aren't ready, then I have to stay away." It hurt to even say the words, let alone keep himself on the couch.

"I don't think you have to."

"What are you saying, Shaye?" His question came out sharp unintentionally. He needed her to be clear.

She sat down beside him and took in a slow breath. "I already chose you. I came back for the bear. I did that. I came back for you." Her hands lay in her lap and he watched her spine slowly straighten. The colour of her eyes deepened, pleading with him to believe her.

"Final decision. I need to hear it. I won't force you to be stuck with me."

She nodded. "Final decision."

His grip tightened around his beer bottle until he feared it would break. He set it down on the end table and stood. That was the moment he lost his control. Nathan bent and lifted Shaye off the couch and threw her over his shoulder. She yelped and gripped his shirt in tight fists to avoid falling. She wasn't going anywhere.

His body heated and every inch of skin crawled. Sparks lit up his spine. He knew his eyes weren't their own when he dropped her on the bed and she gasped, staring directly at them. He shamelessly trapped her in his gaze. Her acceptance was all he needed. The patience wasn't within his capabilities to ask her again.

Nathan ran his tongue along his teeth. They had already grown and sharpened in anticipation of marking her. The call echoed within him. *My mate. Mark her. Claim her.*

She seemed frozen in place as he rid himself of his

clothes. It was a good thing he didn't care about the shirt of his she was wearing. Nathan grabbed her wrist and pulled her up. Once she was on two feet, he gripped the front of the t-shirt and pulled, ripping the soft fabric to bare her skin. Her nipples were stiff and he growled, bending his head to capture one in his mouth. He wrapped an arm around her back to keep her from falling as he bent her over. Even those tasted exotic.

He laid her back on the bed and followed her down. He captured the opposite nipple and savoured her small moans. This time, she would scream his name. No quiet climaxes for her.

His t-shirt lay forgotten in pieces beneath her and over her shoulders. Nathan moved down her body, licking, sucking, and tracing patterns with his tongue. When he reached her core, he grinned knowing how sweet she tasted. His mouth watered.

"Nathan?" He couldn't tell if she was begging or if she was uncertain of what he would do. It didn't matter. He set his mouth to her clit and rubbed over it roughly with his tongue. Her hips bucked back, but he quickly moved his hands to her hips to hold her in place so he could draw circles around the nub. Probing her entrance, he pushed two fingers inside, stretching her. He groaned with her heat. Fuck, he needed all of her. He needed to make this quick.

Lifting his head, he replaced his mouth with his thumb. He played until he had the right position, the right pattern, and the right pressure. Her muscles tensed and her breathing was stilted.

"Don't hold back on me, sweetness." He moved his eyes down her body. Her clit was engorged beneath his thumb. "I'm going to watch your cunt come. Come for me, Shaye. Let me hear it. Let me see it."

Her entire body shuddered and her walls tightened. She let out soft moans on short breaths and he watched juices leak out around his fingers.

"That wasn't enough. I need more of you." He leaned forward and clamped his mouth around her clit, knowing it would be over sensitized while she was still coming down from her orgasm. She cried out and tried to pull away. He gripped her hip and sucked while he flicked his tongue directly over her clit. It only took seconds for her to come again, her cries echoing around the room this time. He worked her down and finally lifted, moving himself up her body. "That's more like it."

He sealed their lips as he thrust into her. Her body, although weak, came alive beneath him. He heard the call again. *Mate. Mark. Claim.* Nathan lifted his head and caught her gaze. She had to know that this was it. He wouldn't be able to stop it, but he wouldn't surprise her.

Feeling his orgasm rise from the base of his spine, he picked up his pace to chase the pleasure just out of his reach. Their breaths mingled and their eyes collided and trapped the others. This was it. His. She would finally be his. Truly his.

His climax gathered in his balls and shot upward. Nathan growled, but in his ears it sounded like he roared. He spilled himself inside her. Sliding a hand behind her head, he fisted her hair. He pulled her to the side and buried his face in her neck. Instincts were there to take over for him. He bit her, piercing her soft skin. Her taste, her scent, her essence invaded every part of his system. A new wave of pleasure crashed through him and into her like a rough wave. A second orgasm hit him, and she shuddered just before he felt her heat clamp and convulse around him.

Her cry was the sweetest sound and ended with his name whispered in his ear.

He licked and kissed the small wounds on her shoulder until they faded. "Mine," he murmured low and nipped her ear before losing his strength and collapsing on top of her.

SHAYE'S BODY didn't feel like her own. New sensations, new feelings, overwhelmed her, firing through her veins. She took a long time to come down from the high in which Nathan forced her. It was the most euphoric state she'd ever experienced.

Finally, his weight on top of her registered. He lifted off and pulled himself out, eliciting a groan from each of them. His hand in her hair loosened and he stretched his arm to wrap around her. He collapsed beside her and curled his arm, pulling her against him.

"Thank you, sweetness." His chest rumbled with his husky words. Shaye hadn't told him, but she loved when he called her that.

Shaye waited for the regret to set in. She meant what she said to Nathan, but she still resented Fate for Her hand in everything. Once she realized that Gwen was right and she needed to figure out if she would have chosen him under normal circumstances, she could see it. To see how obvious it was all along.

She drifted off to sleep, huddled in his warmth. But Nathan was restless. Sleep wouldn't last long.

Nathan woke her with his fingers. He massaged her breast, pulling the nipple between his thumb and forefinger. She gasped, her eyes fluttering open to find bright brown orbs looking down at her.

"I'm sorry. I can't stop." His apology sounded pained. Shaye didn't intend on complaining. Just his touch had her body ready for him. She threw her head back and allowed herself to feel it all. It wasn't just his touch or the desire she could feel. There was more. Emotions, maybe not even hers, were throbbing within her. It was overwhelming, and it created a strong pull into her core.

His hand travelled down her body while his mouth claimed her. She could get lost in his kiss alone, but she gave him her breath when he guided his fingers inside her. He curved them and brought her to the peak, her nerves still sensitive from the last three orgasms he gave her. She held herself back from going over the edge. It happened too fast.

She felt him smile against her lips. "That's how you want to play? So be it." He removed his fingers and moved above her. She didn't have time to adjust before he thrust in. He didn't give her mercy. She felt every inch of him. There was too much and not enough. "That's it. Give it all to me, Shaye."

He buried his face in the opposite side of her neck and bit. Warmth, heat, pleasure. It all invaded her system and forced her body to the end. She came with a moan she didn't recognize.

Shaye felt his seed spill inside her. Damn it. They should talk about that, but her thoughts wouldn't stay focused. Now wasn't the time, anyway.

She sighed as he rolled them to their sides and let her fall into a proper sleep. One she needed. She lost too much of it over the past couple days.

SHAYE INVITED Nathan to her place for dinner the next day, offering to cook for him. The change in her filled him with relief. The dark circles beneath her eyes had disappeared and the slump in her shoulders straightened. She was brighter and happier when she left his place for work.

"How was your day?" Nathan followed her into her kitchen and took the onion from her to dice. She smiled and he caught sight of the woman he found alone at the lake.

"Not a struggle. The past couple days have been hard to get through. I'm expected to have a certain demeanour and mood. It wasn't in me. Today felt much better." Shaye turned on the oven to preheat, then took the meat out of the fridge.

"Good." Nathan stopped her when she passed him. He placed a chaste kiss before letting her go. Her returning smile was all he needed.

"What about yours?"

"Not much changes in my days. People don't talk to me at work to begin with. They really won't talk to me when I'm obviously in a foul mood."

"People don't talk to you?" She set the meat in the baking dish and turned on him, curiosity between her eyes.

"I'm not a talker."

Shaye tilted her head. "You're the grumpy man that lives alone in the woods." Her lips struggled to stay straight.

"Exactly." He didn't have a problem with his description. He kind of liked it.

Content settled between them since the night before. Things were where they were meant to be, but Nathan knew there was more. He wasn't willing to do or say anything more. He had her. She was marked as his. That was the best he would get for now.

They finished eating and Nathan couldn't hold back. He had to have his hands on her. The poor woman would never get a break from him. He didn't need to speak for her to know what he wanted from her. He watched her pupils dilate and her pulse quicken. The base of her neck throbbed and he could hear her heart. Everything he experienced, she did too through the mate bond. Sometimes, he'd wondered if Asher and Gwen exaggerated. They hadn't, and he and Shaye had only begun.

He leaned across the table and cupped the back of her neck to pull her forward. He kissed her, moving his lips over hers and tracing each with his tongue before pushing it inside.

A knock on her front door interrupted them. He hoped the footsteps he'd heard hadn't been on their way to Shaye's door. He growled as he pulled away. Shaye looked a little dazed. She licked her lips and seemed to recover herself.

Nathan followed her out and leaned against her mantle above the old fireplace in her living room. Crossing his arms, he sniffed, recognizing her friends' scents. He filled with satisfaction at having claimed Shaye as his. She was his, not theirs. He had to remind himself they meant well, but it didn't dissolve them from treating Shaye the way they had.

Shaye opened her door and her friends walked past her into the house, although with less enthusiasm than Nathan would imagine.

"Hey, Shaye. We hadn't seen you in a while and wanted to come hang out if you weren't busy." Jenna stopped beside her, but the two guys walked further in and frowned when they caught sight of Nathan. One of them tapped Jenna on the elbow. She turned and her eyes widened when she saw him. "Oh, you have company."

"Yes, I do." Shaye paused, and Nathan knew she was working through her thoughts regarding her friends. She closed the front door and stepped in front of him. "This is Nathan. Nathan, these are my friends. Jenna, Jerry, and Chase."

Sticking true to his grumpy-man-who-lives-alone-in-the-woods persona, Nathan stayed where he was until Jerry stepped forward with his hand extended. Although, his frown didn't disappear. Nathan shook his hand, then looked at Chase. Hesitantly, Chase extended his and Nathan shook it.

Her friends were all close in age to Shaye, but seemed so much younger. Some of what Shay had told him about them made sense now. They held the maturity level that was expected of an early twenty-something, but Shaye had lived more, grew up quickly with a necessary independence. He didn't notice the age gap between him and Shaye. He noticed it between him and her friends.

"You're welcome to stay for a bit." Shaye started talking to her friends and Nathan went back to lean against the mantle, not interested. He looked over the pictures that sat there. A wedding picture from over twenty years ago. Pictures of Shaye as a little girl and another of her graduation. Some alone, some with whom he assumed was her father. A small, aged, golden frame stuck out from behind the wedding picture. Nathan pulled it out.

Two men stood with their arms around each other's shoulders. The men looked young, maybe twenty, if that. One was the same man in the rest of the pictures, Shaye's father. But the other had Nathan frowning. He looked familiar.

All the air left his lungs and his grip tightened. The other man looked like him. Too much like him. He'd seen this picture before. The frame cracked in his hand.

"Nathan?" Citrus and pine appeared beside him and his lungs filled again. His mate steadied him. "Everything okay?"

"Yeah," he croaked. He set the picture back where he found it, but had to lean it against the wall for it to stand now that he broke it.

Her friends stayed, arranging themselves on Shaye's furniture. Nathan followed Shaye into the kitchen. She started to clean up their dishes. Nathan touched her shoulder to stop her.

"I got this. Go hang out."

"You sure?"

"It will only take a minute and I'll be right there." Nathan kissed her. She went to the fridge and pulled out a few beer, holding the necks of the bottles between her fingers. Nathan listened in on their conversation while he cleaned up.

"That's the same guy from the pub the other night, right?" Jenna asked.

"Yup."

"Who is he?" One of the guys asked.

"I told you. His name is Nathan."

"Where does he work, Shaye? What does he do?" Impatience dripped from his voice.

"He works at the lumber yard."

"How did you meet him? And when?" Jenna's voice was calmer than the guys. They seemed to still feel protective of Shaye. Nathan couldn't blame anyone for looking out for her, but they were going about it the wrong way. He knew Shaye wouldn't put up with it much longer.

There was a pause before Shaye answered Jenna. "I went back to the lake after our camping trip. I met him there." Nathan smiled to himself. Her answer was accurate enough.

"You went back alone?" It was the other guy that asked

this time. Nathan wasn't sure which was speaking yet. No answer came. "Sorry," he mumbled. *Good girl, sweetness.*

"Is it serious?" Jenna's voice dropped. Nathan froze on his way to the sink. This answer he wanted to hear. Would she openly admit what their relationship was? Shaye paused longer than he'd like.

"Yeah. It is." Nathan sighed. He finished up in the kitchen while Shaye attempted to change the subject to focus on her friends.

When he walked back into the living room, conversation halted. His gaze drifted to Shaye's mantle, where the picture hid. The picture and face weren't just familiar. He knew without a doubt he'd seen that exact picture before. But where and when was what he couldn't remember.

CHAPTER 12

Shaye woke before Nathan the next morning. She crept out of bed thinking she made it out without waking him, but she realized that was impossible with a shifter.

"It's too fucking early, woman." The pillow muffled his groan.

"I know it is, but I'm up this early every morning. Out of necessity, I swear." Shaye disappeared into her bathroom to shower and get ready for work.

She wasn't sure what to make of the previous night. Mostly, her friends had been on their best behaviour. They disapproved of her going back to the lake without telling them, and they disapproved of Nathan. Even Jenna, although she tried hard not to show it. Hopefully, they would all come around with time.

Then there was Nathan. He'd been distracted, not that he hadn't been contributing much to the conversation, and no one had attempted to include him either. But Shaye often found him focusing elsewhere in the room, and toward the pictures she had of her dad. He saw something in one of them. Something that caused a big enough reaction he broke the frame in his hand. It was still together and leaning against the wall, but it was lopsided. She needed to talk to him about it this morning.

She finished in her shower and dried off, then used the towel to wrap around her hair. She stepped out and straight to her closet.

"Mmm," Nathan hummed in appreciation, which had been her intention when she walked out of the bathroom naked. She sent a sassy smile over her shoulder. He'd propped himself on one elbow, his eyes raking over her body, only briefly meeting her face. If she didn't hurry and get dressed, she would be late for work.

She pulled out a pencil skirt and a loose blouse and set them on the bed. His eyes heated her skin. Shaye picked up her pace. Pulling out underwear from her drawer, she put them on then grabbed a bra. When she turned around to get dressed. He smirked. Her reaction was clear as day to him.

"You're cute when you're flustered."

"I'm thinking you did that on purpose." She put on her blouse and started on the buttons.

"As did you." The corners of his eyes crinkled. He climbed off the bed. Shaye couldn't stop herself from taking the time for her own perusal of his perfect body. He lifted her chin and devoured her with a single kiss. Then he turned around so she had a view of his perfect ass as he walked into the bathroom.

Shaye sighed. Her body heated further, and she didn't have time for this. She finished dressing and took the towel from her hair. She followed him into the bathroom to blow dry it. She bent over and flipped her hair upside down to dry it quicker. When she flipped it back and stood, Nathan stood in front of her, water droplets running down his skin and a towel hung low on his hips.

Shaye wanted to lick each drop of water from his skin. They ran down, all coming together below his hips. His taste invaded her memory. She licked her lips, craving his taste on her tongue.

She shook her head. "Nope. No. Can't. No time," she muttered to herself and walked around him while shielding her eyes. His laugh echoed out of the bathroom and the rich sound fed the inferno building inside her. And the bastard knew it too.

Waiting in the living room alone helped calm her body. But as soon as he walked down the stairs, she started all over again. Outside. They needed to get outside and around other people. Shaye hated the smile that played on his lips. He had to be feeling the same attraction she was, but instead of getting overwhelmed, he was enjoying it.

"Let's go get coffee." She opened the door and left without waiting for him. Once he passed, she locked her door. "Do you know the little shop down the street?"

Nathan pulled a face. "Woods is better."

"We'll have to meet there. We both need our trucks."

"That's fine." He took the four steps toward her and kissed her. It was quick, but it still stoked her body. He got in his truck and waited for her to do the same. She followed him to *Woods Bistro*. When they went inside, Gwen stood behind the counter.

"Hey, you two."

"Hi," said Shaye. Nathan only nodded, but his smile was friendly. "I didn't know you worked here."

"I started the same time I met Asher. However, this is my last week. Nathan, I like seeing you inside instead of just through the drive-through." Gwen eyed him suspiciously, but her lips were twitching. Nathan shrugged. "Well, what can I get you guys?"

"Your dark roast, please," Nathan said, then looked at Shaye for her to order.

"Cappuccino, please."

Gwen gave them their total and Nathan paid. They said goodbye to Gwen and took their coffees outside. They sat on one of the benches outside of the bistro. Neither of them could stay long, both needing to get to work, but Shaye didn't want to dash away so soon.

"What picture had you distracted last night?"

"You noticed that, did you?" He sighed. "I'm sorry I broke the frame."

"That's okay," she said softly.

"It was a picture of your father and another man, both very young. I've seen that picture before." He frowned at the white cup in his hands. The struggle to search his own memory was plain to see.

"How?"

"I don't know. It's the man standing with your father. He's familiar. And I know I've seen that exact picture. But it must have been a very long time ago."

"I'll look at it tonight after work and see if I can tell you who he is." Shaye laid her hand on his leg and squeezed. She wasn't sure why it felt important to help him. It could be nothing. Just someone who resembled someone from his past. But the way he stared at it last night told her it meant something to him that even he didn't know. She'd look at the picture and if there was anything more they could look into about it, they would.

But she needed him to open up more about his past. Something he seemed reluctant to do.

NATHAN WAS MORE than distracted throughout the day. The picture, Shaye, his bitter life. His thoughts jumped from one to the other. His frustrations built. He never had this kind of difficulty concentrating. He wasn't the type of person to have wandering thoughts.

Compartments he had buried deep in his memory shook as the images inside poked their doors, trying to get out. Things moved around in his mind that Nathan didn't want touched. Digging up his past only brought to light more of his curse. If it turned out to be a blessing, something else always had to give. There was a consequence to every blessing out there. And he wondered what consequence there would be now that he had his mate.

He wanted to forget he ever saw that picture.

Nathan pulled into Shaye's driveway and had to wait for Shaye. He sent her a text to tell her he was here. Her response came quick. She was finishing up and would be on her way. Nathan leaned his head back against the headrest and closed his eyes.

They had barely begun their relationship, but things would change for both of them and rather quickly. He hoped Shaye was ready for it. Nathan wouldn't fight it. He didn't want to fight it. He may not have wanted to find his mate, but he wouldn't change anything now that he had her.

Soon enough, Shaye parked her truck beside his. He got out and met her at her front door. Before she unlocked the door, Nathan grabbed her shoulders and turned her to face him. His mouth crashed down on hers with more intensity than he planned. The sight of her after being separated for the day spurred his need. His heart pounded and started a new rhythm in hers. His cock throbbed and he smelled her arousal and heat growing to match his. Their bodies fed off each other.

They stood on her front porch while Nathan devoured her mouth. His arm wrapped around her back and the other took her keys from her hand. Shaye placed her hands on his chest. He enjoyed the heat that penetrated him from her palms and each fingertip. Without breaking their kiss, he unlocked her door. He dropped her keys back in her bag, and tightened his arm to lift her off the ground.

Nathan walked them into her house and slammed the door. Her hands frantically moved up his chest and over his shoulders. One hand broke away and moved down his side and traced the waist of his jeans. His cock jumped, eager to play.

Nathan let his body do as it pleased. He let the bond between the two of them create and play out its own desires. Their instincts controlled this now.

He started to undo the buttons of her blouse, but his fingers fumbled over themselves in his haste. Inwardly he cursed and ripped the blouse open, buttons popping and dropping to the floor. Shaye gasped and Nathan nipped her lip. He pulled at her skirt to bunch it up over her hips and she started pulling at his belt. Neither of them had graceful motions in their rush to get beneath their clothes.

Nathan pushed her back against the door. He reached between her legs and pulled the damp fabric of her panties to the side. He ran his fingers through her silken lips and groaned. She had his pants undone and his cock free. Her tiny hand wrapped around him and he just about came. She squeezed and stroked her hand up to the tip.

The growl crawling up his centre demanded freedom, forcing him to break the kiss. He bent his knees and grabbed her below her ass and lifted. Her legs wrapped around his waist, opening her up and at the perfect angle. Rocking his hips, the head of his cock found her entrance.

He thrust slowly until he sunk in an inch. But that was the most patience he could muster. He thrust home, slamming her against the door. Her hands delved into his hair and gripped, holding herself against him. The pricks of pain only added to his urgency. He panted and buried his face in her neck while her heat engulfed him.

Sweat rolled down his back. He changed his grip and slid one hand up her side until he cupped her breast.

He worried about the bruises he'd leave on her body, but it wasn't enough to stop him. Pleasure raced through him until it culminated at the base of his spine. Dizziness swamped his head and his climax shot upward from his balls to the tip of his cock in a quick rush. Her walls clamped onto him in the same instant and her body turned rigid in his arms. Her soft moans blew into his ears.

The entire scene was uncontrollable pleasure, desire, and purely selfish on his part.

"I'm sorry, Shaye." Nathan pulled out and slid her down to the floor. Her knees buckled when he released her. He wrapped his arm around her and pulled her against him, off the hard surface of the door.

"Huh?" Her dazed eyes tried to focus on him. Dilated pupils, thin hazel rims. Beautiful in the aftermath.

"That was inappropriate."

The slow lift to her lips reminded him of the mischievous cubs he and Bear grew up with. "I like inappropriate." Some of his guilt lifted, and he leaned his forehead against hers while they finished catching their breath.

"How about some food? And then maybe we can do some more inappropriate things." Nathan slid his fingers through her swollen, sensitive folds, enjoying her sharp intake of breath. He flicked her clit and she jumped before he settled her panties over her pussy.

They helped each other with their clothes and made their way into the house.

Nathan froze when his eyes landed on the mantle covered with pictures. The euphoric warmth that had bubbled under his skin turned cold. He wished he could ignore the issue that image created, but he knew it would haunt him until he dealt with it. And what worried him more was it would invade their relationship. It was another piece that tied them together, but he felt it was also something that could tear them apart.

TREMORS RAN through Shaye until she finally sat down beside Nathan to eat. She took Nathan out to her BBQ and put him to work while she made the salad and dressing. Now, they sat outside on her deck to eat. The burgers were her own creation that she kept in the freezer. Satisfaction brought a smile to her face when she heard him hum over the first bite.

"What do you put in these?" he said around a mouthful of food.

"Secret recipe." It wasn't, but she liked to tease him.

"I'll find out some day."

The wind picked up as they finished eating. It whistled through the rails on her deck. Shaye gathered their empty dishes and took them inside, but Nathan didn't follow. She cleaned up and thought about going back out with him, but turned into the living room.

Her father chose most of the pictures on the mantle. Shaye added her own as she grew, and more after her father passed away. The one that fixated Nathan was small and had been put there by her father. It had been there for as long as she remembered. Its position overrun by family photos over the years.

She pulled the broken frame off the mantle, careful when lifting it from its place. She clasped it with two hands to keep it from falling apart. Her dad looked so young in this picture. It had been about the time he met her mom. Shaye had to think about the other man in the picture. It wasn't anyone she met growing up, but the way her father had his arm wrapped around him, she knew he'd been important. Her memory jarred with a faint echo of her father's voice. She'd asked about this picture before. Looking up at the mantle, she saw the picture of the first fish she ever caught sitting in front of where this one had been. She remembered her dad lifting her so she could place it on the mantle herself. That was when she'd asked about this one. Her head tilted as she eyed the picture and her dad's voice filled her memory. But as the man's name dawned on her, she scowled. It was the surname that caught her attention.

Shaye turned around to go back out to Nathan, cradling the frame in both hands. She stopped short when he walked in from the kitchen.

"I was wondering where you went." His hand ran down from her shoulder to her elbow, spreading warmth.

"Nathan," she paused. She needed to tell him. It might be nothing and only a coincidence, but that wasn't likely. He looked down at her hands.

"You've been looking at the picture."

"Yes. This one has been up there since before I can remember. But I also remember my dad telling me about it. His name is Damien Marks."

Nathan staggered back, then took the picture from Shaye.

"They were best friends growing up. But my dad always

looked sad when he talked about him, so I asked him one day what happened to him. I was still little, so I'm sure he gave me a censored version."

"What happened?" Nathan's voice sounded hoarse.

"He told me Damien made some bad friends and turned into a bad person. He said that when they got older, Damien came back to my dad for help because he wanted to be a good person again. Said he'd met someone and fell in love."

"Then what happened to him?" Nathan's motionless eyes locked on the picture.

"I don't know, but he said they, I assume whatever group he was with, came after him one day." Shaye could only give him the story as told to a little girl. Her adult mind had to put the pieces together. "Was he your dad?"

Nathan only nodded. "I have to go. Will you come with me?"

"Of course."

He set the picture down and grabbed her wrist, pulling her to the door. She grabbed her bag that still sat on the floor near the entrance, but Nathan didn't stop until they stepped outside. He allowed her enough time to lock up then pulled her along again.

He drove toward his house, keeping the truck just enough above the speed limit that most cops would still consider acceptable. Nathan hit the brakes, skidding to a stop and hopped out. Shaye followed, but froze after she closed the door. A bear that looked identical to Nathan stood in front of his house.

Nathan walked right past him as if he didn't notice the large animal. Shaye followed him, but took cautious steps, not wanting to spook the bear. Nathan must have realized she wasn't behind him because he appeared in the doorway.

"That's Bear. He won't hurt you." Some urgency seemed

to have left him now that he was in his own home. "When I first shifted, I was matched, or paired, with a cub. He's like my animal twin. We're identical."

"Do all shifters have one?" Shaye tentatively reached her hand out. Bear tilted his head, then looked at Nathan. When Nathan nodded to him, he stepped forward and allowed Shaye to touch him.

"All the shifters I've met do. Come on in. I'll introduce the two of you better later."

Shaye ran her fingers through his fur one last time and followed Nathan. She felt the urgency in him returning.

His house wasn't big, so it surprised her it had an attic, although it was only the size of a crawl space. Nathan's feet still stood on the top of the ladder while he rummaged around. She heard boxes being moved. He pulled one out and passed it down to her. "Can you take this?"

Shaye lifted her arms. It wasn't as heavy as she expected. By the time she straightened from setting it on the floor, he passed the next one down to her. There were four boxes total. Nathan carried the last down as he stepped down the ladder. He walked to his living room, so Shaye picked up a box and followed. Nathan did a second trip to bring the last two.

He tore into the boxes, only looking at things briefly before setting them aside. Pictures, papers, books, trinkets, and medals covered the floor.

"What are you looking for?"

"The picture."

Shaye opened the next box and sorted through it. About halfway through his box, Nathan spoke.

"Found it." He held an unframed picture between his fingers, the edges tattered. "I knew I saw that exact picture before."

"There's writing on the back." Shaye pointed at the back of the picture. Nathan turned it over and read the inscription.

"Joseph Nathan Tierney and Damien Adam Marks. More than friends." Nathan looked up at Shaye. His eyes clouded. "Your father's middle name was Nathan?"

"Yeah, it was," she whispered.

"I wish your father was alive so he could tell me what happened."

"Me too." Shaye's eyes watered.

"Shit. I'm sorry, sweetness." Nathan cupped her cheek and ran his thumb over her lips. Even with sadness in her heart, the move sent a sliver of heat through her body.

"It's okay." She locked eyes with him. Regret formed in her heart, but she didn't understand why. It didn't come from her moment of grief over her father. It was Nathan's. "There has to be someone that knew both of them. Maybe there's someone else that could tell us what happened."

"Yeah." He nodded and searched through the piles he'd made when looking for the picture.

His regret grew and echoed within her. She helped him search. Anything to ease the pain. Questions hovered on her tongue, but she waited. He wasn't ready.

CHAPTER 13

He'd been a kid the first time he'd gone through the boxes in the shack he and his mom lived in. Then he'd sorted and repacked it all when he'd finally left. He hadn't known what any of it meant. He'd kept papers he thought might someday be important and anything with a name. Everything else were things he thought looked cool. It was all junk now. Except the things of his mother's that he stored himself when he cleaned out the house. The few pieces of jewelry she still owned, trinkets, her journal.

Her journal.

Nathan ran back to the crawl space. He pulled out the last box he had stored. The one he kept his mother's things in. Separate. Separate from the things of his father who Nathan blamed for everything. Those men came for him and killed his mother. Her things wouldn't ever touch his. But now he had to dig through his past to discover what happened to his father. Because that would explain what happened to his mother.

He set the box down amongst the others with extra care.

Nathan had to force himself to pull in a breath. Going through this box would be harder. This one would bring memories to the surface.

"What's in that box?"

He couldn't answer Shaye. He opened the box and pulled things out, not giving them his attention, focused only on his mother's journal. When he found the purple faux leather cover, he wrapped his fingers around it and pulled it out. He passed the journal to Shaye and repacked his mother's box, cupping each item as he would his mother's hand. Not looking at the crystal rocking horse, her tiny wooden jewelry box, the tiny teddy bear he gave her for her birthday the year she died. He pushed the box away after closing the flaps, closing the memories back inside.

"Your mother's journal?" Shaye sat cross-legged with the journal open in her lap. Nathan could see his mother's handwriting. He used to ask her what it meant because the letters didn't look like the ones he'd been learning. She promised she would teach him cursive writing one day. He'd learned on his own.

"Yeah." He nodded. "I'm not sure if I can read it." His voice cracked, and he had to get up to get a drink. Water should have been enough, but he grabbed a couple beer instead. He didn't care the alcohol didn't affect him. He chugged half of his down before going back into the living room.

When he returned, Shaye's concentration was on his mother's stories, emotions, life. He didn't know what she wrote about, but she had written in it every night. Those were the things he remembered most, the things that stayed the same. She must have had more than just one. To write every night would fill the pages fast. But he didn't see others when he cleaned out the house.

He passed Shaye the beer, dangling the bottle in her peripheral vision. She looked up and took it.

"Do you know how old you were when your father was gone?"

"Two, I think."

"This journal starts from your second birthday. The first entry is the only one that mentions him."

"Can you read it to me?" If Nathan read it himself, his mother's voice would echo in his head. He never planned on going through any of this again, happy enough to move on and just be. But a damn picture that haunted him pulled him in, and now he couldn't let it go. He couldn't let his mother go.

Shaye nodded slowly. He watched her lips embrace the tip of the bottle. She took in a breath after she swallowed and read his mother's words.

"I won't say much about this because it doesn't matter anymore. Staying strong, healthy, and alive is what's important. For my son. Keeping him strong and healthy. Raising him to be a strong man. We're alone and it's all up to me. I'm scared. I don't know what happened to Damien. Not exactly. I'm not stupid. I can put it all together. He's gone. The sound was unmistakable. I don't know why. I don't know who. And I don't know where his body is. But like I said, it doesn't matter anymore.

I ran. I packed the bare minimum and Nathan and I ran. I don't make a lot of money. I wouldn't have been able to support us in the house we were in. I found a place we can call home. We're hidden and we'll be happy, eventually.

Today is Nathan's birthday. He's two. He misses his daddy and doesn't understand. But being two, he's happy. We will be just fine.

I made him a cake. We ate half the icing before I could get it on the cake. I gave him a library card and a toy truck for his birthday. He's hugging both of them while he sleeps beside me.

I will remember this day. I might remember sadness in myself, but I will remember how happy he was. Every minute of the day was exciting for him. The special pancakes for breakfast, the walk to the park, the playground, his presents, and a movie.

And that is exactly how I want him to remember every day."

Nathan tilted his beer back and emptied the bottle. He'd thought by listening to Shaye read aloud he wouldn't hear his mother, but he was wrong. It felt like she was sitting beside him and reading him a story. He remembered that library card and truck. He didn't remember getting them, but those were two of his most prized possessions.

The journal entry didn't tell him any more about what had happened or why, but it explained why they had been living in that shack.

"Are you okay?" Shaye's soft question brought him out of his past. He turned his head toward her. Her bland expression didn't hide the emotions inside her. They mirrored his own and reflected back and forth between them. An odd sensation burned in his gut from the confusing mixture.

"I don't know. Nothing can change the past. I would rather let this all go. It won't make a difference now and I don't need it."

"Did you ever grieve?"

"I never knew how and by the time I did, the time had passed." Animals grieved, but emotions weren't complicated for them. He spent four years as an animal. Four years living as a bear cub before he had to face the life he had. Before he had to face the memories. Life was simpler that way. His grief had been simple and short.

"Grief isn't linear or logical."

"I've opened all these boxes. I'm not sure if I can let it go even though that's what I want to do. Maybe I should have burned it all years ago. There would be nothing to drag me into it now."

"You would have regretted doing that."

"But I wouldn't be stuck searching through a person's life. A person I don't care about." His body itched and his frustrations grew. He didn't want to be in his own body anymore.

Nathan stood and pulled his shirt over his head and tossed it on the couch, then unfastened his jeans. He pulled them down his legs and laid them over his shirt. Shaye stood, still clutching the journal in her hands.

He stepped over the piles on the floor and wrapped a hand around her nape. "I'm sorry, but I need to go run." He pressed his lips to her forehead and drew in her scent. He carried it with him outside and while he shifted. Bear quickly showed up by his side, ready for whatever Nathan needed. He looked back at the house and saw Shaye leaning against the door, understanding reflected in her eyes.

He was lucky Fate gave him the mate She did.

SHAYE WATCHED the two bears run deeper into the woods. His pain leaving a trail behind him. This would not be easy. He needed to grieve, but he fought it. She didn't blame him for wanting to fight it and push it all away, thinking it would just be easier to never dig deep into the past. But it will rot his mind and soul if he didn't get closure. Shaye was thankful she didn't allow her grief to consume her, although it had been a close call.

She didn't think he grieved his father, but grieved the idea of a dad. He hated him too much for leaving his mother, no matter how he left.

She didn't want to be the one to push him into dealing with the past. He needed to tell someone what had happened, and he needed to find out why. Shaye would need help. She would stand beside him as his mate.

For now, she cleaned up the piles they made from the boxes. As she picked through the papers, she wrote down any names she found before putting it all away. Maybe the people were insignificant. Maybe they could shed some light. Or maybe they were the exact people that took his father and mother away from Nathan.

She stacked the boxes by the ladder to the attic that Nathan left extended. The box of his mother's being the last one she moved. She couldn't put it in the same pile, seeing how Nathan had cradled the box and the items within. She set it a few feet away and laid her journal on top. They needed the journal and that box for him to heal.

Shaye stepped outside and looked around, hoping to see two big bears barrelling toward the house, but nothing appeared. Silence engulfed the woods except for an owl hooting and the sounds of water sloshing in the lake from the wind. She sighed and shut the door. It was getting late, and she still had to work in the morning.

She welcomed the shower as a respite from the harrowing emotions. She reminded herself she needed to talk more with Gwen about the bond and how it changes mates. A physical connection formed between her and Nathan, one she wasn't sure what to do with.

She used his shampoo and body wash, then rinsed. Pulling one of his t-shirts on, she checked at the front door one more time for the return of the bears before going to bed. She understood his need to get out. Get out from behind walls, get out of her own skin. In his case, literally out of his own skin. When she went camping, she was running away from her own mind and her own world. Shifting did that for Nathan. Of course it would. He spent years doing that as a child because he didn't know any other way to survive.

Curled up on Nathan's side of his bed, she breathed him in. His scent stronger and more distinct. It settled her body and allowed her to sleep. She woke easily when she heard Nathan outside. She listened to his footsteps up the stairs. He opened the door and tried to shut it quietly, but the click and small thump was still loud in the house.

Shaye sat up in bed and waited, tracking the sound of his bare feet padding through the house. He went straight to the bathroom and turned on the shower. She thought about following him in there, but gave him as much time alone as he might need. If he wanted company, he would come to her.

When he walked into the bedroom after a quick shower, a few water droplets still lingered on his skin. They were just as tempting now as they had been that morning.

He looked different. He felt different. An aura she recognized surrounded him. Freedom. He lived it. And she suddenly saw she didn't have enough of it. Sure, she enjoyed her job, but it consumed her. If it wasn't her job, it was her friends, who's behavior had been turning protective without her realizing. She always imagined what it would be like to let it all go and live the way she truly wanted in her heart.

Shaye put herself up on her knees and pulled his shirt off. Nathan stopped just inside the bedroom door to watch her. She stood beside the bed. His eyes turned molten, deepening in colour and flashing bright across the dark room. He walked toward her with slow and purposeful steps. A new edge encompassed him. His sharp arousal jumped off his skin and ran along hers. Her nipples tightened and her core clenched. All from him, running across the physical tie between them.

As soon as he reached her, he dropped the towel and reached for her. Shaye dropped out of his grasp, sitting on the edge of the bed. She looked up at him and licked her lips. Her hand wrapped around the base of his cock.

She explored his length with lazy strokes. Leaning forward, she licked away the water running down beside his naval. Muscles beneath her tongue twitched and his cock jumped in her hand. It was more than enough encouragement for her to do it again to the few other droplets she found making their way down toward the treat she held in her hand.

With nothing left to lick, Shaye continued down until her tongue tickled the base below her hand. Nathan's body was hard in front of her. He barely breathed, standing like a perfect statue for her to enjoy. She wanted to give him the slow, torturous pleasure he deserved.

Shaye circled the tip of her tongue around the head. She wouldn't take him into her mouth until he squirmed, ready to do it for her. She gently sucked in the head, then traced it with her tongue again.

"What are you trying to do, sweetness?" Amusement laced his unrestrained growl that vibrated through her body. The sound of his voice was delicious and enough to have her walls throbbing in eagerness for him to have his revenge on her. He made her wild.

"What does it look like I'm doing?" she asked sweetly.

"Trying to kill me is what it looks like."

Shaye allowed her plan to shine in her eyes, and she added her hand back into her work. He didn't last near as long as she'd hoped.

"Shaye." A warning whipped through his growl, and his muscles trembled. She moved her hand to the base and opened wider. She sucked him in until he hit the back of her throat. Bobbing her head, she worked on him harder than she had any other man. She didn't know what she did that was different, but her desire to please him was higher. The craving to taste him was higher. He was important to her. And that made all the difference.

His cock swelled inside her mouth and Nathan roared. He ripped her hand away and his delved into her hair and pulled her head back. He followed her with his hips and tilted himself over her.

She made him lose control, and she loved it. He thrust, his cock going down her elongated throat each time. Pain prickled her scalp with his unrelenting grip. She couldn't move, couldn't suck. She could only swallow him down. He fucked her mouth until he finally froze buried inside her mouth. Warm spurts of salty liquid shot down her throat while he panted and growled above her, his thrusts quick and short.

His grip loosened and he dragged himself out. Her fingers rose to touch her swollen lips. Nathan's jaw worked up and down, but he said nothing. His nostrils flared and his eyes looked wild. She brought out the beast and couldn't wait to see what he would do.

THE TINY WOMAN in front of him stripped him bare. And he let it happen. He was speechless. He was raw.

He looked down at her perched on his bed. Blonde hair and hazel eyes. She glowed. He saw the mark on her shoulder throb. The call to mark her again roared within him. He intended to pay her back for the slow torture, but tonight wouldn't be the night.

His cock hardened again and his body was ready to claim what was his. Maybe he could squeeze in a bit of payback.

"On your hands and knees," he demanded. Her eyes widened, but she didn't move. "Now, Shaye."

Slowly, she moved herself into place, her knees near the edge of the bed. He ran his hand up her spine. When he reached her neck, he pushed her down toward the bed creating a better angle. One that would allow him to go deeper.

Placing both hands on her hips, he worked his cock into her heat. Shaye took shallow breaths until he made it all the way in, then she stopped breathing altogether. He didn't want her to adjust to his invasion. He started a grueling pace. When her walls tightened around him, he reached one hand around to find her clit. He placed one finger over the hood and pressed while he stroked up and down. Shaye pushed her hips back to meet his, chasing the pleasure he promised to give.

It wasn't easy, but he held back his own orgasm while hers built. He had to grit his teeth and focus on only her. The sounds she made, her body's reactions, sensitive skin. Her hands fisting the sheets above her head. Her cunt was slick, and he easily slid in and out, but her muscles tensed. He couldn't allow himself to pay attention to his own rising pleasure.

Finally, she broke beneath him. He rode her through the contractions of her climax, making it last. When her shudders eased, he pulled out and allowed her to collapse onto the bed. He grinned to himself. No rest for the wicked.

Nathan rolled her over and hooked her leg over his arm. Her eyes opened as he probed again at her entrance. She cried out as he pushed in with ease, scraping over her sensitive tissues.

"You've taught me something, sweetness. Torture is fun." Nathan covered her clit with the heel of his palm and applied pressure until she groaned. It didn't take long to push her over the edge. A fact he was thankful for. It was becoming more difficult to hold himself back. But he still wasn't done with her yet. "Again."

Nathan tilted his hips to hit her sweet spot inside and bent his head to suck in a nipple. Using his teeth, he grazed the erect pebble. His fingers played with her other breast, kneading over the mound to pinch the peak. Shaye went wild beneath him, but his weight kept her where he wanted.

Her walls tightened unbearably around him. This time, he let himself go with her, but not until her orgasm had taken over her body.

He released her nipple and buried his face in her neck, waiting. His teeth sharpened as he pumped in and out of her body. Finally, she came apart beneath him. As soon as his own orgasm began, he bit into her shoulder, devouring her taste. The mark sent fresh waves of pleasure through each of them.

He licked and kissed the mark on her shoulder while both of their bodies quaked.

With barely enough strength to manage, Nathan lifted himself up and got a cloth to clean them off. He tossed the cloth in the hamper and tucked them in bed, wrapping his body around hers. She fit into the curve of his perfectly.

Everything in him was overwhelmed. They were growing as a mated couple. The bond was strong. He felt strong. She did that for him. And he did it for her. As much as he hated to admit it, maybe Fate knew what She was doing.

CHAPTER 14

Exhaustion still clung to Shaye when she got to work. They picked up coffee on the way and she poured herself another from the office as soon as she arrived. She needed the boost. She didn't function well on only a few hours of sleep. At least she didn't need a boost in her mood. It didn't matter that they had filled their night with searching through his past. It ended in the most delicious way. With pleasurable torture for both of them.

Her hand hovered over her shoulder, above the new mark. The light coloured crescent wasn't obvious. It could pass as a birthmark, until someone saw the matching one on her other shoulder. Shaye shrugged and let it go. With nothing she could do, she wondered if she would change how things were now.

Their souls connected on a primal level that each understood. She was drawn to the wilderness and Nathan was the epitome of wild.

"Shaye, I need you to set up viewings for these houses. Back-to-back, please, then cycle through again for a second client." Her boss set a list down on Shaye's desk.

"Sure thing."

"And you're coming with me," she called from her office door.

Shaye sighed. It would be a busy couple of days.

After making the appointments, she checked to make sure Diana had left the office and gave Nathan a quick call. He finally answered just before she gave up and hung up the phone.

"Hey, sweetness." She felt like a goof when her smile broke across her face at his gruff greeting.

"Hi. I'm going to have a busy couple days starting this afternoon. I just wanted to let you know I'll be late tonight. I have to attend back-to-back viewings, then do the same list of viewings again tomorrow."

"You work for a busy agent."

"I work for the top agent in Alder Ridge."

"Come to my place when you're done?" he asked. Shaye only hesitated for a moment until she realized that spending the night without him wasn't what she wanted.

"Okay."

"Good. See you tonight."

"See you tonight," she echoed.

She got to work sorting files. They had five houses to show. The client for today was a young newlywed couple that came into their office about a week ago. They both had amazing jobs and wanted to secure a home before settling down any further and having kids. They were living life in order.

Fate must favour them. Maybe they weren't fun to fuck with. Or, Shaye thought, maybe Fate fucked with the ones She loved.

Shaye had everything together by the time Diana returned from lunch. "We're starting early. I've added two more to our schedule. I just need to grab those files." Her boss dashed to her office. When she came back with the files in her hand, she kept a brisk pace out of the office and to her car. As normal, Shaye worked her shorter legs a little harder to keep up with her. It's why it was rare for her to wear heels. Those things just made it down right difficult.

Her afternoon was exhausting. They showed every type of house available since the clients didn't know what they were looking for. They went from a bungalow, to an acreage, to a duplex, to a farm-style, and a few others. Shaye discovered the clients were particular. Forcing her mind to hold polite thoughts ensured her professionalism shone through to the clients. Particular wasn't what she would prefer to use to describe the couple.

Her feet hurt and a headache formed at the front of her head when they reached the last house. A large white family home on the edge of town, sitting on an acre of land. Green shutters, trim, and door made the house stand out. A beautiful yard had two large old trees in the front yard and space for gardens and a shed in the back. The fenced in property provided a sense of security and privacy.

The sight alone spoke of a warm welcome. Shaye opened the file. The home was over thirty years old, empty for most of its life. The extensive renovations had been recent. This was practically a brand new house, and one of Diana's recently acquired listings.

Shaye skimmed over the sellers' details, how long they'd owned it, when the renovations had been completed, what inspections had been done. But she did a double take over the personal information. She also dropped the folder on the lawn when the name finally registered.

Damien Marks.

Her breathing picked up, and she felt rage and panic

build. She looked up and remembered where she was and who she was with. Shaye couldn't do this now, couldn't allow emotions to reign.

She looked up at the house and allowed one last thought before focusing on the clients. Was she about to walk into Nathan's home?

NATHAN'S EYES narrowed on Shaye as soon as she walked through the door. Her eyes avoided his, but it wasn't a deliberate move. Something distracted her. A scent of panic lingered, emanating from her neck.

"Shaye?"

She shook her head and looked up, a smile on her lips but not in her eyes. "Hi."

"Something wrong?"

She pursed her lips and took a slow breath through her nose. "I want to tell you no. I want to pretend everything is fine. But I'm not so sure it is."

A sickness settled in the pit of his stomach. It originated from Shaye. What she felt from whatever she had to say projected into him through the mate bond. He walked over to her and wrapped his hands around her waist. "What is it?" He bent his head to look into her eyes.

"The last house on the viewing list for a client today was recently acquired by my boss. It's over thirty years old, empty for most of it, and extensive renovations. He's our client, so his information is in the file." She paused and Nathan froze with her, dread building with her next words. "The owner is Damien Marks."

"*Was* Damien Marks."

"No, Nathan. *Is.*"

"That can't be right."

"I'm sorry I don't have an explanation for you. That is the owner's name on the house."

Pure rage and hatred boiled inside him. The fucker was alive? His mother died for him. Thought he'd been killed. She did her best thinking he had been taken from them, not abandoned them.

Nathan had a decision to make. He had to decide what to do with this information. His choices swirled in his mind. Turning away from Shaye, he tried to lay them out. He could continue down the path of answering the questions to his mother's death and no further. He could see what his father had to say for himself. Or he could go on a fucking man hunt. Nathan's heart hardened. His eyes heated. He knew they looked vicious.

The answer seemed simple. He would do all three.

"Nathan?" Shaye's soft question turned him back around. She gasped and stepped back. He closed his eyes and shook his head. Taking in a deep breath, he filled his body with the scent of his mate. It calmed his soul. Relief reflected in her when he opened his eyes.

"Sorry, sweetness."

"What are you going to do?"

"A lot of things. But nothing that can't wait for tonight." Nathan didn't want to chase this too hard. He wanted the answers. He wanted his father's head. But he would not jeopardize the life Fate had given him to do it. It was the past, and he'd always been happy to leave the past where it was. Until recently.

He planned to introduce Shaye to Bear tonight. He hadn't explained everything about himself and knew he needed to soon. The bomb she brought into the house didn't need to halt anything.

"Have you eaten?"

"Yeah. We grabbed something after the viewings."

"Good. Come with me." He took her hand and pulled her back outside. Once on the ground, Nathan inhaled, pulling in the scents from the trees and the lake. "Bear!" he yelled. His ears picked up the crunch of his footsteps. Nathan watched Shaye. It surprised him to see her turn her head in the direction Bear was coming from long before he was in view. Her senses were improving from the mate bond. Gwen told them all that it happened to her and they continued to sharpen.

He smiled. This life suited Shaye.

Bear came around the side of the house and stopped a few feet away from them. "This is Bear. I'm sorry I haven't told you much of him before. I was in a rush."

"That's okay." Her voice gentled. He heard the touch of nerves he'd expect. Her reaction similar to when she first met him by the lake.

"He is a real bear, not a shifter, but he's different. He won't hurt you. As bears, we're identical." He turned her toward the lake and Bear followed along too, walking just ahead of them. "His mother found me. She saved me. She took me home with her, to her cub, Bear. They took me in as a boy. I fell asleep before anything happened. I remember seeing the wind around me and I remember its warmth as it ran over me, but I fell asleep before I first shifted. I woke up the next morning as a bear cub. He changed too. His growth slowed. It took us a long time to grow from cubs to full grown bears. His strength and abilities match mine. The only difference is, he can't shift."

"What did his mother save you from?" Shaye looked up at him then turned her gaze back to Bear, releasing the pressure for him to answer.

"The men that killed my mother." He didn't have a reason not to answer her, but the words were strange coming out of his mouth. Nathan had never spoken to them before. He'd told no one, except Bear. Shaye stopped and grabbed his arm.

"Oh, Nathan. You were only four."

Bear paused and looked over his shoulder when he noticed they'd stopped walking.

Nathan nodded. "I wish I could tell you I didn't see it happen, but I did." They stood surrounded by trees while Shaye shook in front of him. He felt her determination. He wasn't sure if it was determination to not cry for him, or determination to go after the bastards. Maybe it was both. He knew he felt both himself. Always had. "Bear's mother stormed into the house before they killed me too. She waited while I laid with my mother, hoping she'd wake up. I was four. I didn't understand."

"Oh God, Nathan. I am so sorry."

He shrugged. "This life is a blessing and a curse, remember?"

"No, Nathan. Your life is a blessing. It's someone else's curse that took your mother."

Neither of them had to voice who shouldered the curse. Rage built again at the thought of his name. But what relief would Nathan get if he pursued him?

Nathan stepped back from Shaye and stripped. He laid his clothes by a tree and shifted, needing to run off the anger, run with Bear, run with his mate. He couldn't stand to lose the life he had, and he wouldn't be stupid enough to put it in jeopardy.

SHAYE IGNORED the frown on Diana's face when she skipped out of the last viewing the next day. It didn't matter they weren't certain of the owner's identity. Her emotions shot upward just looking at the house baby Nathan might have been torn from due to the actions of his father. Fate didn't work in coincidences.

She took a snapshot of the seller's information. If Diana found out, she could be fired over it. They could find the information on their own, but they might as well skip a few steps.

Shaye's ears pricked and she put her phone away and followed the click of Diana's heals.

"Shaye. Is there a reason you need to leave early?" Early was relative. This was working late, but Diana considered it early because they weren't finished. Shaye never had a problem with that, but tonight was different.

"Yes, I'm sorry. Something's come up."

"Care to share?" Her eyebrows rose. Her boss had a tendency to be nosy. Shaye rarely shared information with her. She preferred to keep her career separate from her personal life.

"No." Shaye smiled and left the office. She drove straight to Nathan's and arrived before him.

She got out of her truck and saw Bear lying in the grass. Bear stood and Shaye walked over to him.

"Hi, Bear." She still felt nervous around him. It was odd to spend time with a dangerous animal. It might have begun to feel normal with Nathan, but it wasn't. And now she had to get used to Bear. Nathan had said they were identical. She should treat Bear the same way she treated Nathan.

She reached out and tentatively ran her hands over his head. He closed his eyes and leaned his head into her hand.

"You and Nathan are basically brothers, aren't you?"

Bear looked up, then he gave a short nod. Shaye smiled.

"I like it when an animal answers me. Do you know how many questions I asked Nathan when I thought he was just a bear that he could have answered, but never did?"

Bear nudged his head under her hand again, put out she stopped touching him.

"I don't think the next little while will be easy on him." Shaye worried about what he would do. Bear stilled, then his head bobbed. He understood. Most likely more than she did. He'd lived through it with him. "He has us. He'll be fine. Right?"

Bear leaned against her and she draped her arm around him. He followed her to the steps, and she sat while they waited for Nathan to come home. Nathan hadn't locked his house. Shaye could go inside if she wanted, but spending time out here with Bear was comforting. And she felt he enjoyed the company.

Nathan pulled up a few minutes later. He smiled when he got out of the truck. "Looks like you two are getting to know each other well." Bear laid his head on Shaye's shoulder. "No, Bear. She's mine, not yours."

Bear huffed, his hot breath blowing in her ear and moving her hair. Shaye giggled. Bear lifted his head as Nathan neared and he helped her stand.

"I have something to show you." She pulled out her phone and opened the picture. Turning it around, she showed him, watching his face change as he took in the information. An invisible hard ball hit her and her body heated with anger. She looked up and Nathan stared at her, his eyes flashing. His emotions, his anger at his father had hit her.

He closed his eyes and took a deep breath through his nose. The anger receded as he opened his eyes.

"I'm sorry about that."

"It's okay. I just didn't realize I could feel so much from you."

"It's the mate bond." He ran the back of his knuckles over her cheek and down her neck, heating her skin in another way.

"What do you want to do?" she asked to distract from her body's reaction. It wouldn't stop them from what they would do once they went to bed, but it might keep them from jumping each other right this moment.

"Research first. I won't do anything that will put you in danger."

Shaye softened. He was a true protector but hadn't had anyone to protect. Maybe Bear while growing up, but he took care of himself now.

"I'll start tonight. But I want to spend time with you first." His voice dropped, and he closed what little space was left between them. Bending, he lifted her. Her legs wrapped around his waist instinctively and he carried her inside. So much for waiting until later to let their bodies and emotions rule.

CHAPTER 15

Nathan crawled out of bed in the early hours of the morning. Shaye slept sprawled on her stomach. The sheets covered up to her waist and what skin that showed gave off an aura that beckoned him. She was the most precious thing to him. He needed to remember that. All he wanted was answers. For now. Damien Marks would not know Nathan knew he existed or where to find him. That was assuming his father knew he was alive. Nathan had been an adult before he claimed his identity. The last thing he had wanted growing up had been to get taken away from Bear and Auntie. He saw what it did to Zachary and Smoke. He could only imagine the pain a child would be in with that separation.

Answers. Nothing more tonight. Find the man, spy on him for a little while, and that's it.

Shaye stirred and lifted herself up on her elbows. Nathan leaned down and placed a kiss on her head, intending to leave, but she rolled and wrapped her arms around his neck. She pulled him down for a kiss and he allowed her. "Be careful." Her sleepy voice made it difficult for him to leave.

He stood and she rolled back over to her stomach. He strode out of the house, not bothering with clothes. Spying on anyone looking like a man was too risky.

Once outside, he shifted and Bear met up with him near the lake as they'd agreed. They nodded at each other and started off through the woods. Nathan had his address memorized. And the address of the house he's selling. They would check out both of them.

Trees surrounded Alder Ridge with more wilderness running through it. It made for a great place for shifters to hide in plain sight to travel through town.

The house up for sale stood in an older part of town and looked like one of the better houses there. At least it looked that way now. Many of the others were well lived in and in need of a bit of repair. Some face lifts and a few renovations to make the homes look happy again. He'd been through this neighborhood countless times. The big white house didn't spark any memories. He didn't expect it to. He hadn't even been two years old.

There was nothing to find there. They moved further into the woods and went to his current address, which was just outside of town in an expensive looking suburb that seemed to be its own complex. The houses were large, modern designs and all similar, although the exteriors were different colours. Only a few had decorated or landscaped lawns.

Nathan and Bear split up to walk around the outskirts. Wire fences skirted the community.

Nathan inhaled, searching for what he could scent in each house. Everything was faint and well mixed with so many others. He found the address of Damien Marks.

Nathan crouched down in the woods behind his house and listened.

Bear found him and hid beside him. They waited. Nothing more to do. He would rather storm into the house to find his answers, but all he had to do was think of Shaye to stop himself.

An hour before sunrise, they heard movement and two figures stepped out onto the back deck. One an older man wearing only sweats and the other a woman most likely younger than Shaye, dressed in only a bra and thong. His hand wrapped around her throat and he kissed her, forcefully. She leaned into him, but he suddenly broke the kiss and shoved her away, his only grip on her neck. Two men came from the side of the house and grabbed her, covering her mouth before she even knew she should scream.

The older man leaned on the railing with his elbows. Nathan smelled disgust flowing from him through the air.

The house has guards. As do most of the others. Bear said beside him.

I noticed that. Shaye said his dad got in with the wrong people, bad people. Nathan wondered just how bad. His mother had been positive he'd been dead. The man on the deck resembled the picture, but he was much older, making it difficult to be sure. How was Nathan going to confirm if that man was his father? No, if he was Damien Marks. The events around his disappearance and life since didn't matter. He'd started this life putting his future in danger before it even existed. He was still to blame. Nathan could never forgive his mother's murder. The nightmares of a four-year-old boy still haunted him. He still cried out for her to wake up. He had put the blanket around her when Auntie buried her, hoping it would warm her up enough to wake.

Damien puts those events in motion. He might as well have pulled the trigger.

Nathan. The sounds of Bear in his mind made him shake his head. *You need to calm down.*

Sorry. Nathan turned his thoughts away from the past and focused only on the information he wanted. They watched nothing happen for another couple hours until Nathan had to leave to get to work.

I'll stay.

No. Nathan turned on Bear. *I won't have you getting hurt without me here. I'm not losing you.* Bear's eyes widened in surprise at his vehemence.

Okay.

Nathan sighed and started the hike back through the trees. Bear was just as important to him as Shaye.

Movement on the back deck caught their attention. They crouched low and listened.

"Jacob wants to schedule shipment for three packages. One per week starting next week." A guy dressed in jeans and a black t-shirt sat in one of the deck chairs. The presumable Damien stood over him.

"What are the packages?"

"He doesn't want to say." The guy tilted his head back.

"Too bad. He knows my rules."

The other man shrugged. "I'll tell him again, but he was adamant the contents were confidential."

"Then he knows I won't ship them. What else is on the docket?" Damien moved to the edge of the deck and looked into the woods, directly over Nathan and Bear.

"Tyler has a shipment of coke he wants taken through the mountains. The girl you shipped off this morning is secure and on her way. And Jason wants a meeting."

"Then let's go meet him." Both men walked back inside the house.

Nathan's stomach turned, having figured out what the man did. And sadly, he'd heard of them before. He just never knew the names of the people running it. It looked like Damien ran the shipping company. He had his information to start with. Nathan needed to get out of there before he did something stupid.

Shaye was sick with worry. Nathan and Bear didn't make it back before she had to leave for work. The unknown drove her mind to madness, so she stopped off at *Woods Bistro* for coffee on the way to work, hoping Gwen would be there. She was working the front.

"Hey, Shaye," Gwen said as Shaye approached the counter.

"Hi, Gwen." Shaye looked around her before facing Gwen. She leaned forward as if to whisper. "Do you have a minute?"

"Sure." She stepped back and asked another girl to cover for her and came out from around the counter. "Is everything all right?"

"I think so. Would I know if something is wrong?" She felt silly asking, but the mate bond was strong enough she often felt Nathan's emotions. It might not be such a far-fetched idea.

"What do you mean?" Gwen pointed to an empty table. They both sat before Shaye continued.

"How far does the mate bond extend? Would I know if something is wrong with Nathan?"

"Oh," she said when understanding donned on her. "Yes,

you probably would. I did, and it turned out it wasn't even as big of an emergency as I assumed. Why do you ask?"

"I don't know where Nathan and Bear are. They left in the middle of the night and didn't get back before I had to leave this morning."

"Where did they go in the middle of the night?" Gwen asked.

Shaye hesitated. "Does Nathan share much with the other shifters? Do you guys know what happened to him?"

"No. I've been trying to get him to tell us his story since we met. I'm keeping a log, creating a book of legends, about everything we learn and each shifter's story. There's so much we don't know, and future generations won't know either if we don't keep track."

"Then he probably wouldn't want me saying anything, would he?"

Gwen tilted her head and pressed her lips together. "Probably not." She sighed. "But back to your question. If you don't feel uncontrollable panic, he's most likely fine. Try calling the lumber yard to see if he showed up for work."

"Good idea." Shaye liked Gwen, and she was someone who understood everything she was going through. "Gwen, would you like to meet for lunch?"

"Today?" Her eyebrows rose in surprise. Shaye supposed the invite was sudden.

"Yeah." She needed another friend these days.

"I'd love to."

"Great. I'll come back at lunch and we'll go from here." Shaye stood and Gwen followed.

"I can't wait."

Feeling a little lighter, Shaye went to work, capable of acting like the chipper, friendly person she was. Diana was late coming into work, which wasn't odd, but she usually called Shaye first. Shaye shrugged and started sorting through messages at her desk.

Half an hour later, her boss came in, an excited bounce in her stride. "The Jennings couple from two days ago are interested in the Marks house, the white family home in the older neighborhood. I'm taking them to see a couple more that are similar, but it sounds like they are leaning toward that. It's just the neighborhood that's making them second guess. Can you put the neighborhood information together while I'm out with them? Maybe see what type of neighbors are around, school proximities, those sorts of things."

"Of course." Most of that information they usually had, but where the house had had no one living in it, some of those questions had been left blank. It was also a new listing. Sometimes they needed time for their research.

Shaye forced herself to treat it like any other house, like any other sale. They weren't certain if the Damien Marks that owned the house was also Nathan's father. Deep down, the truth was there, but until they confirmed it, she had to keep moving forward as if life was normal.

A sense of happiness came with an inward grin. Life would never be normal for Shaye again. Her life was becoming a wild entity, and she loved it.

She gathered what information she could from the office then spent her last hour before lunch driving through the neighborhood. It had an eclectic age dynamic which created a great environment. Older couples walked hand in hand, teenagers played basketball in their driveways, and young families sat outside with toddlers running in the grass. The look of the older houses showed nothing of the neighborhood's character. It was a beautiful place to start out and raise a family one day. As Shaye imagined it was thirty years ago.

Parking her truck, she took a walk around the block, noting the playground and green spaces available. There were walking trails, and every neighbor held a smile for her, the stranger.

"Beautiful day," an older lady said as she passed with her husband.

"It is. And a beautiful neighborhood. I don't often come through here." Shaye smiled gently to encourage conversation.

"Oh, this is a great area to live in." The pride was evident in her tone.

"How long have you lived here?" Shaye asked. The couple stopped, looking eager to make conversation.

"At least fifty years, dear. Have lived right across from that empty house. Wasn't always empty. It's been a sad sight. I look forward to when it's sold, and a growing family is living there once again."

Shaye couldn't help herself. The information was available here in front of her and it must be for a reason. Fate and her puzzle pieces. "Do you remember who lived there last?"

"I do," she said, sadness etched in the lines on her face. "Not sure what happened. He left or disappeared, and she took the baby and ran away. I watched her frantically pack her little car, leaving so many things behind. The house sat like that for years."

"That's a shame." Shaye not only hurt for Nathan, but for his mother too.

"It sure is. A sweet family. Not without their problems, but what couple doesn't have those." She waved her hand in the air as if pushing everyone's marital problems into their own compartment of life.

"Do you remember their names?"

"Marks. Now, I'm not sure I remember his name, but the mother's was Audrey and the baby..." She paused and touched her husband's arm. "Do you remember their names, dear?"

"Nathan. Father was Damien," he answered, and Shaye had her confirmation. And just so she didn't seem odd, she moved in step beside them for their walk and asked a few more questions.

"You've probably seen many families come and go."

"A few. So many families start out expecting to move after a few years, but then they fall in love. We all rely on our neighbors. It's nice being in an older part of town."

She accompanied them back to their home and let her show Shaye her garden before making her excuses to meet Gwen for lunch.

Relief washed over her as she walked into *Woods Bistro*. Her worries had invaded her work life. She had to tell Nathan and she would, but she wasn't sure what he would do. While waiting for Gwen, she called Nathan's cell.

"Hi, sweetness," he answered gruffly.

"Oh, thank God you're okay. I've been worried."

"I'm fine." But she heard the anger in him.

"Did you find out anything?"

"Yeah." Shaye took his silence for not wanting to talk at that moment. That was probably best.

"I'm going to have lunch with Gwen. It shouldn't be a late night at work."

"I'll meet you at home." His home. Shaye should probably check on her own home in the next day or so.

"Okay." There was silence over the line. Something missing. Something unsaid.

"Bye, sweetness."

"Bye." She sighed when she tucked her phone back in her bag.

"Ready?" Gwen's bubbly persona bounced off of Shaye as she came around the counter.

"Let's go." Shaye looked forward to getting to know the other shifter mate.

NATHAN HAD to close his eyes after listening to Shaye tell him what she learned. All the information fit together except two little details. Why did his father leave and why did someone come looking for him and kill his mother? He had everything he needed to move forward, but what he would do was the question. Approaching Damien and making him aware of his existence, making that connection, could put Shaye in danger. Just as Nathan's mother had been. He couldn't live with himself if something happened to her because of his actions. He needed to ask himself to let it go. Take what information he had and move on. Did it really matter why his father left or what he'd gone through?

"Nathan?" Shaye touched his arm. He took a deep breath before he allowed himself to open his eyes. He felt a piece of evil inside his soul grow. It tried to break free and roll through him to spread its hatred.

"Shaye, I don't know what to do." It was difficult to admit, but his choices clashed.

"What's your goal?"

"My goal?" He struggled with the answer despite her simple question. "Before seeing the picture of our fathers, I wanted nothing to do with this. I was fine to leave it as it was. But now it burns." He beat his chest once with his fist. "I'm reliving the horror of my mother's death each day."

"Are answers going to help? Are they going to do anything to ease the pain? Or are they going to make it worse?"

"They'll probably make it worse. And possibly put what I have now in danger." Nathan reached out and with his knuckles resting on her jaw, he ran his thumb over her bottom lip. Heat and desire simmered in each of them. "I won't do anything to risk you. And from what I learned today, Damien is dangerous. He runs the biggest illegal shipping operation through the mountains. I've heard of it. I didn't know who ran it."

Nathan stood from the table and pulled Shaye up. He clasped his hands around her waist and lifted, shifting his grip under her ass.

"Nothing will ever harm you."

She brushed his hair back off his forehead. The light touch of her fingers reminded him of the precious gift he'd been given. "You can't promise that."

"As long as I'm with you, nothing will harm you." He had confidence in the vow he made.

Shaye bent her head and kissed him. Her lips moved slow over his. He drank in her taste, letting it feed his arousal. Two steps out of the kitchen to go to the bedroom and his phone rang. A second later, so did hers.

They both sighed, and he set her down. If it had just been his phone, he would have happily ignored it, but he knew Shaye couldn't ignore hers. She went back to the kitchen to get hers and Nathan pulled his from his pocket.

"Hey."

"Hi. How is everything?" Asher asked. Nathan didn't really have many people call him, but Asher was becoming a common one.

"Fine. I guess."

"You coming to the meeting tomorrow night?" Asher tried to sound like he didn't care, but Nathan knew he did. And Nathan was more willing now to be a part of it. It might still go against the grain, but Nathan knew he needed to be part of it, part of a growing pack. Bears didn't have packs, but it seemed shifters did.

"Yeah, I'll be there."

"Shaye too?"

"If she's not working late, I'll bring her." They said goodbye and hung up. Shaye came back, her face scrunched.

"I have to go to work early in the morning. A couple wants to put an offer on Damien's house."

"There's a meeting at Asher's tomorrow night. You can come if you aren't working." He changed the subject, not wanting to discuss Damien or the house that should have been Nathan's home.

"Of course I'll come." She smiled and stepped back into his arms. All Nathan had to do was feel her skin beneath his hands to calm his emotions. She grounded him.

He lifted her again and carried her to bed. The need to bury himself in her heat, to bring himself back to reality, to what was important to him, was growing. He needed her. He needed his mate.

CHAPTER 16

They took Nathan's truck to Asher's. Bear left ahead of them through the woods. Shaye's head hurt. Hatred toward Damien and his actions in Nathan's life caused conflict inside Shaye. She felt his struggle, and it was difficult for her to look at it objectively.

The Jennings couple put their offer in first thing that morning and Damien soon submitted a counter offer. She felt it was smart of them to wait and consider before putting in another offer, but Shaye saw how much they loved the house and knew that by morning they would repeat the process and hope Damien accepted.

Since Nathan was undecided on what to do with the new information, then so was she. They needed clarity. She didn't know what to expect out of these meetings, but she hoped they found it here.

Nathan parked beside a motorcycle and turned to her. "You ready?"

"Of course."

Nathan huffed and got out of his truck. Shaye followed,

and he waited for her at the front. She tucked her hand in his and he led them to the woods.

She heard voices and something smelled odd as they walked further into the trees. Birds chirping in the trees sounded sharper, a little shrill. Their footsteps on the ground carried a crunching sound she never noticed before. Soon, the scent off the breeze made her nose twitch.

"Wolf."

"What?" she asked, unsure what Nathan was talking about. She already knew the other shifters were wolves.

"That scent. It's wolf."

Gwen warned her about this. The increased senses since Nathan marked her. Gwen explained how in certain situations she could smell and hear with increased ability. She hesitated to say as well as the shifters. Shaye hadn't understood, but she did now. Gwen asked her if she would be comfortable talking about her experiences as a mate for her to record in the legends she was writing. Shaye agreed. Without Gwen, she would be blind in all of this. She would hate for future mates to be just as blind.

She tried to stop the itch in her nose with the strange scent before they met up with the group. They broke through a couple trees and saw a mixed crowd of people and animals. Bear waited for them away from the two wolves, one white and one grey. Like walking in on a fairy tale, the massive animals looked magnificent. With their heads held high, their fur moved slowly with the breeze and their eyes glowed. Gwen stood beside Asher, and they both smiled and waved. And another man stood a little off from the group. He had a deep tan and darker hair. The steel grey eyes told her he belonged to the grey wolf, although powers of deduction made that clear. But what she found odd was that Asher stood beside the white wolf and Nathan moved to stand beside Bear, but the grey wolf stood beside the white away from his shifter. Something wasn't right with them.

"You've met Asher and Gwen." Nathan pointed to the couple standing across from them, then over to the other shifter. "That's Zachary. This is Shaye. My mate."

Zachary nodded to her, and she lifted her hand in return, but was at least polite enough to speak. "Nice to meet you."

"Thanks to Nathan, we have the lumber and a better design for the house." Asher spoke, then looked at Shaye. "I'm building a communal house, a safe haven."

"A headquarters," Zachary interrupted.

"A headquarters," he agreed, "deeper in these woods close to my pair's territory. It will always be stocked with clothes and food and open for shifters, and their mates, whenever they need a safe place."

Shaye liked the idea. Nathan seemed so alone. Now, he had a community on which to rely. Poor man, wanting to be left alone and somehow dragged into all of this. Shaye tried to hide her amusement, imagining Nathan being brought out of his hidden den.

He looked down at her and raised a brow. She had to purse her lips to suppress her giggle.

"Is the foundation finished?" asked Zachary.

"It is. Framework is next."

"Who's building it?" Nathan's gaze switched from her to Asher.

"I am," said Asher.

"By yourself?"

"My dad has been helping when he can, but mostly it's just been me."

"Well, hell. Let's go." Nathan pulled his shirt over his head and everyone looked at him with fierce confusion.

"What the fuck are you doing?" Zachary pushed himself off the tree he leaned against.

"If we're just going to stand here and shoot the shit, we might as well be working on building the house. Let's go." He finished stripping and turned to her, grabbing her chin in one hand. "Do you want to come?"

Shaye looked sideways to Gwen. The other two shifters began undressing, and Asher looked down at his mate, his lips moving with a low tone escaping. Her eyes caught Shaye's, and she nodded to the house.

"I'll stay with Gwen."

"All right." He kissed her. Never were his lips sweet when they touched hers. Raw emotion and power flowed through what would be a chaste kiss for anyone else. A moment of dizziness rushed through her when he released her. She greedily took in the sight of his naked body before he shifted. Looking past the initial pain, she saw the beauty and the magic. When she looked back at the others, the only person left was Gwen. They were surrounded by four wolves and two bears.

The animals ran through the woods, leaving the two women behind.

"Want some wine?" Gwen asked.

"Yes, please." Shaye didn't worry about sounding too eager. She needed some time to relax from the turmoil with Nathan.

THE ANIMALS RACED through the woods, Asher and Kai often playing on the way. Smoke and Zachary ran beside each other, but they still kept their distance. Bear nudged Nathan, and his emotions formed a grin. Seeing the repercussions of the falling out between Smoke and Zachary bothered him, bothered both of them. The sad faces he often saw Gwen sending them said it bothered her too.

But unless Nathan was ready to share his problems, then he couldn't stick his nose into Zachary's.

They all shifted when they made it to the building site. The wolves and Bear wandered off together before splitting up, Kai and Smoke toward their territory and Bear in the opposite direction. Asher threw Nathan and Zachary each a pair of jeans. He pulled them on, then took a walk through to see what Asher had started. He'd done good work so far. Nathan picked up a hammer and a pouch of nails and got to work where Asher had left off. The other two joined him.

"Thanks for the help, Nathan," said Asher as he stepped up next to him.

"There's no point in meeting just to update each other on our lives. We might as well do something while we talk." Nathan caught the twitch on Asher's lips.

"Then let's talk while we work. I noticed you marked Shaye."

"I did."

"Even knowing what to expect when Asher and Gwen mated, it still took me by surprise when you two showed up." Zachary grabbed tools for himself and moved to the other side of the wall. "I'm not sure I want that."

"You don't have a choice." Nathan and Asher replied in unison.

"I won't chase after a mate."

Nathan stopped, letting his arms drop. He waited a moment for the other two men to look at him. "You'll experience unbelievable pain and an uncontrollable shift where your animal instincts will decide for you. That's assuming certain experiences are the same for all of us." As far as mates went, they assumed it was the same for every shifter. Two out of three were good odds.

"You tried to fight it?" asked Asher.

"Before I even smelled her. The wind wouldn't leave me alone and I wouldn't chase a feeling of something off near my home. Because I wouldn't search out the disturbance, I was forced to shift. It was Shaye. She was camping near the lake with her friends."

"I can imagine that was an interesting introduction." Zachary grabbed a nail and adjusted his hammer in his hand.

"She met a bear. She didn't meet *me* until a couple days after." It surprised Nathan the conversation came so easily to him. He didn't mind telling them how he met Shaye or warning Zachary of the consequences of fighting the pull of a mate.

They worked well together, finishing the wall Asher started. Nathan owed Asher. Asher might not think so, but things wouldn't have been so easy when finding Shaye without his and Gwen's help. He considered asking for their help again, but indecision struck Nathan. Inwardly, he sighed and kept working.

"Smoke doesn't want to leave Alder Ridge. Do you plan to move here?" Asher asked Zachary.

"I can't. Not yet." Zachary didn't elaborate. Like Nathan, he seemed to have difficulty sharing his problems.

A screech from the air caught their attention. A large hawk flew low through the trees. It circled back and perched on a branch. With its head tilted, it eyed each of them. All three men sniffed the air.

A second hawk swooped down and joined the first. The

scent of hawk with that special effect and the second that sat next to it made it obvious a shifter and his pair sat above them.

Asher nodded at the two and returned to work. Nathan did the same, but Zachary eyed them himself for a moment before also returning to work. The hawks watched while they worked and talked. But they were careful about the details they divulged. While they didn't worry about discussing that they were shifters, they didn't give away details of where they lived or the location of the pack. And they said nothing of mates.

It would be easy to trust anyone because they're a shifter, and Asher wanted that when he started this, but both Nathan and Zachary warned him against being too trusting. Be open, allow others to find you, but don't give details that someone might use to harm any of us until we learn to trust them. That meant any shifters they met, or shifters that found them, would have to approach the three of them first.

Nathan now considered Asher and Zachary friends, rather than an annoyance. He'd never had a friend. The banter came easier between them. And even though Nathan and Zachary were tight-lipped, trust had formed.

A few minutes later, the hawks left. They watched them fly and swoop around them through the trees before moving higher and farther away.

"Another shifter." They heard the excitement in Asher's voice.

"Looks like it." Zachary agreed.

The sun had moved lower in the sky, its light blocked from the trees. They put their tools away and sat on the edge of the building, their feet touching the ground.

It was now or never if Nathan wanted their help.

"Do you guys know of the illegal shipping company that runs through the mountains? Run by Damien Marks?"

Asher opened his mouth to answer, but he froze and looked at Zachary. Nathan felt the quick rise in rage and turned to look at him too.

"Whatever you do, you stay the fuck away from Damien Marks." He heard the wolf inside him growling through his words. "He and his company might be the middleman, but he isn't without his own evils."

Nathan stood. "What do you know of him?"

"He's fucking shit. Trust me. You don't want him to even know you exist."

"Apparently, he's my father." Nathan saw the shock in Zachary's eyes and could feel it from Asher behind him.

"What do you mean, apparently?" Asher asked, the only calm voice among them.

"He left before I turned two. My mother thought he was dead. I recently learned he's not."

"Does he know who you are?" Zachary took an urgent step forward.

"Not that I know of."

"Keep it that way. And you better make sure he knows nothing about Shaye."

"What do you know?" Nathan narrowed his eyes.

Zachary growled and shucked his pants while beginning to shift. He kicked the jeans off his back paws as he ran away.

"Fuck," Nathan swore.

"I wonder if that has anything to do with Zachary's disappearance." Asher stood beside him.

"I'm betting it does. I'm learning that Fate is too much of a bitch to let coincidences happen." Nathan had to roll his shoulders to stave off the change crawling up his back. More secrets, more information he didn't get to know. But were the answers that important to him?

NATHAN WAS QUIETER than usual on the way home. Either from something that happened while they were in the woods, or it was from Shaye's current state. Maybe both. The phone call she got while the guys were working unsettled her. Of course he'd be able to feel it. She needed to tell him. She wanted to tell him. But her growing nerves built a wall to hide behind.

"Say it, Shaye."

"You first." She could use their voo-doo mate magic too.

"Zachary knows something about Damien Marks," he murmured.

"My boss called. I have to take the paperwork to Damien in the morning for the sale. He accepted the last offer."

"You aren't going."

"It's my job."

"Shaye," his voice softened, "Your emotions are inside me. You're scared to go. You aren't going."

"I don't have a choice."

"Zachary warned me it was best if Damien didn't know I existed, if he doesn't already know. He also said to make sure he knows nothing of you. I watched him ship off a young woman just this morning to a place I doubt even Fate is aware of."

"I have no reason to tell my boss I can't do it."

"Call in sick."

"She'll know it's a lie. I'm never sick and she just talked to me on the phone an hour ago. I have to go."

Nathan's knuckles turned white on the steering wheel,

and Shaye wondered if he would break it. He had the strength for it.

He slammed on the breaks, throwing Shaye forward into the locked seat belt. He put the truck in reverse and backed up the lane to return to Asher's. He parked behind the motorcycle.

"We're waiting for Zachary to get back."

Asher and Gwen stepped outside. "Something wrong?" Asher called.

"Yeah. I need Zachary to talk." Nathan sat on the seat of Zachary's motorcycle and crossed his arms. Asher walked over. "Damien Marks is selling a house. Shaye has to take the paperwork for the sale to him tomorrow morning. I need to know what Zachary knows."

Asher let out a long sigh and rubbed his chin. "You might not get it."

Nathan's face hardened. Asher invited them inside to wait, but Nathan refused to even answer him, but told Shaye to get comfortable. She let Gwen pour her another glass of wine and they sat on the deck.

With any other man, it would surprise Shaye how still and strong Nathan held himself for two hours. Finally, Zachary emerged from the trees, but stopped short when his eyes caught sight of Nathan sitting on his bike.

"Get the fuck off." His growl drifted through the air. Asher came back outside and all three of them walked across the yard. Instinct gave a clear warning to avoid the tension building between the shifters, but Shaye ignored it. This involved her and her job.

"I need answers." Nathan sounded calm, but they all knew he wasn't.

"Find them somewhere else." Zachary stopped in front

of Nathan, trying to tower over the man that more than matched his size and strength.

Faster than Shaye could follow his motions, Nathan stood and pulled his fist back. He swung, hitting Zachary across the jaw. His head flew to the side, but his balance never faltered. With as much strength as Nathan put behind the punch, Zachary had in taking it.

Zachary straightened. His eyes flashed almost silver. Asher took a step forward but didn't make it in time for Nathan to throw the next punch. Zachary saw it coming this time and blocked it, but Nathan followed through with another to his gut. Zachary hunched, then straightened almost immediately after.

"I'm not letting you leave until you tell me what you know about Damien Marks."

"What I know is that you should stay as far away from him as possible." Zachary followed his words with a punch of his own. Nathan braced his foot behind him to take the blow when his block missed.

"You two need to stop."

"Fuck off, Asher." Both men growled and turned their glowing eyes on Asher. Loud popping sounds echoed from each of them. Their teeth sharpened beneath their growling mouths.

Grey, brown, and white winds rushed from the trees followed by the animals.

"What has Damien Marks done to you?"

"I don't need to tell you shit."

"Yes, you do. Shaye has to go see him tomorrow. He's sold his house, and she's taking him the paperwork. So yes, you do need to tell me since you've also told me I need to keep Shaye away from him and I can't do that."

"Fuck!" Zachary snapped and turned away. "You can't let her go."

"I have to," Shaye said quietly.

"So, tell me what you know." Nathan spoke slowly through his teeth. The urge to shift seemed to recede for the moment.

Zachary's gaze landed on Smoke, his eyes glazed, then he turned them back on Nathan. "I can't."

"You fucking asshole." Nathan took a menacing step forward, but Zachary held up a hand to stop him. Everyone froze, waiting to see what Zachary would say next. Shaye only realized then that Gwen had a death grip on her hand and they both vibrated with worry. Asher stood ahead of them, but didn't block them.

"I can get into his compound." Zachary's eyes closed. "I'll keep an eye on her, but she can't let on that she knows me."

"Why would you be able to get into his compound?" Nathan's body grew. Even Shaye felt the intimidation it was meant to create. A shiver ran down her spine and she decided that squeezing Gwen's hand back sounded like a good idea. Asher took a step closer to the other men, and Shaye could feel his emotions change with Zachary's revelation.

"Because I can. But you better be in the woods to watch over her too." Zachary pointed his finger in the air toward Nathan. "If things go to hell, remember they have guns before you decide it's a good idea for a grizzly bear to charge over the fence."

"I'm still waiting for an explanation." Shaye saw Nathan's fists shake at his sides.

"You're one to talk." Zachary looked at Shaye. "What time are you scheduled to be there in the morning?"

"Eight." An hour earlier than she would normally have to

be at the office. And that was the time she had to be at Damien's.

"I'll be there. Don't look at me or talk to me."

"I won't," she whispered.

All eyes turned on Nathan. His chest rose and fell with his angry breaths. Slowly his body deflated. "I'm not looking to bring my father back into my life. He was never a part of it. I thought I needed answers. My mother was killed in front of me when I was four by someone looking for him. She thought he was dead. There was nothing she could have done."

"He doesn't have any reason to hurt Shaye, or worse. She'll be there to complete a transaction he instigated. She should be fine. Then you can move on without ever making contact." Zachary was slowly calming down too. It was as if the shifters fed off each other's emotions. When one was angry, anger grew in those around him. Shaye made a mental note to talk to Gwen about that later.

First, she needed to get through a meeting with a deadly man who was the father of her mate and her own father's long lost best friend.

CHAPTER 17

Nathan choked on his fear, genuine fear. Something that hadn't existed inside him in a long time. He was coming to grips with the idea of letting his past all go. The answers didn't matter. To him, it was simple. Shaye just had to refuse to go, make her boss go herself, or send someone else. But there was no one else to send and Shaye enjoyed her job, so she didn't want to do anything to jeopardize her independence. The thought of locking her up in his house for the day crossed his mind. But he wouldn't do anything that caused her to hate him.

He parked beside Shaye's truck, but he didn't get out. "Shaye." He wanted to try again to convince her to stay home.

"Nathan, you need to stop. And you need to calm down. I know you're scared. I can feel it. I was scared enough on my own, but now I'm terrified with your emotions weighing on me too. Everything will be fine. He can't hurt me if he wants to sell his house. If something happens to me while I'm there, the paperwork won't go through."

"You're being naive, Shaye. All he has to do is call your

boss and say you never showed up. Poof. You've disappeared and she prints out the paperwork again and goes herself." Nathan saw the acceptance in her eyes. She already knew the truth, but was in denial. He imagined himself sitting in the woods watching it happen, unable to do anything to save her.

A growl rolled up from his gut. He'd been trying to hold it back, but it punched its way up, gripping his insides to climb. The grizzly sounding growl echoed in the cab of his truck and he slammed his hand against the steering wheel. He got out of the truck. Shaye slowly followed.

He looked at her and her fear was as tangible as his, touchable through the air between them. He couldn't let her go into that meeting tomorrow like this. It wouldn't matter how well she acted, they would see how nervous she was. Nathan had to get a hold of himself. Hide his own fear from her. He wasn't sure if that was possible between mates.

He took several deep breaths as he closed the distance between them. "Zachary will be there, although I'm not sure I trust him. And I'll be near with Bear."

"I think I trust Zachary."

"Time will tell." Nathan wrapped his arms around her and pulled her against him. The warmth of her body soothed the tension in his, giving him a distraction.

Silence reigned while their bodies talked to each. His hands moved up and down her sides and her fingers dug into his chest. For once their heads weren't in this, but that didn't matter right now. Fresh desire and an urgent need were building in his core. He felt the same brewing in Shaye. He bent and rested his chin on her head and closed his eyes.

It was more than desire and arousal rising. It was a connection of souls. A tie was being woven through him and into her and back. Now was as good a time as any to be honest with her, and himself.

"I love you, Shaye." He whispered the words over her hair. She lifted her head, forcing him to raise his. Her jaw dropped open and her eyes searched his.

"I... So fast?"

Nathan didn't respond. After searching his eyes, hers changed. They shone with a gleam of tears. She blinked them back.

"It's true. How can you so soon?"

"Tell me you don't." He threw out the challenge and watched her struggle.

"I can't tell you that," she whispered.

"Then say it, sweetness. I want to hear it."

"I love you, Nathan."

"That's my girl." He claimed her mouth, letting loose every emotion coursing through him, urging her to do the same so he could drink it in. Her hands wrapped around the back of his neck and she delved her fingers into his hair.

His cock rose to attention, ready and eager to rush this along. She gasped and tried to pull back, but he refused to allow any space between them. He would not let go of her until he absolutely had to. Taking her inside would have been the better choice, but he lifted her and carried to the back of his truck.

He lowered the tailgate and leaned against it, his ass barely sitting on the edge. Setting her down, he worked on her shorts to push them over her hips. Shaye wiggled to help get them down her legs, then kicked them away with her sandals. Her frantic hands pulled awkwardly at his t-shirt. Nathan lifted it over his head, giving her what she wanted. She groaned as her hands devoured his bare skin. Little fires struck his skin from her fingers.

He grabbed the back of her neck and pulled her forward for a kiss while his other hand worked on his fly. As soon as his cock was free, his hands found the smooth skin of her hips and he lifted her, bringing her legs around his waist.

"Nathan?" His name on her lips went straight to his cock.

"Hold on, sweetness." He lined up his cock, feeling the slickness over his head. Shaye gripped his shoulders and locked her ankles behind him. With his hand on her hips, he pulled her down, filling her in one thrust.

She'd wear his bruises as he used his hold on her to lift her up and down, her wetness easing the way.

Warmth ruffled his hair, and he looked around them. Auburn swirls circled them and he heard a vow enter his mind. He looked at Shaye, who was following the wind with amazement, then her eyes locked with his. She shuddered as they both raced to the peak and the wind danced faster above them.

Their foreheads touched, and it surprised Nathan she spoke the same vow as him, their quiet voices merging. "Bound and blessed by Fate and wind."

Their orgasms climbed and crashed against each other. Nathan buried his face and sank his teeth into her shoulder. His body throbbed in time with her climax, and his own. She cried out and melted against him, forcing him to change his grip to catch her.

Sealed. Their bond was sealed. Fate couldn't be so much of a bitch to bring them together only to tear her away with danger She created. Could She?

SHAYE WOKE LONG BEFORE DAWN, unable to sleep. In her heart she knew what last night had meant for her and

Nathan. She hadn't been ready, but that didn't make her fight it. She couldn't tell him she didn't love him and she couldn't stop the waterfall of emotions and sensations. Floating on another plain, she felt every part of Nathan as the wind had connected them more than physically possible.

Nathan's fingers lazily stroked over her chest and arms. "You need more sleep." His groggy voice was rough in her ear.

"I won't get it." Thoughts of their relationship then thoughts of her upcoming meeting with Damien Marks would keep her awake. "Besides, there isn't that much time left until I have to go home to get ready. I've run out of clothes here."

"I'll come with you." Nathan braced himself to get out of bed, but Shaye pushed back on his chest.

"No. You need to leave from here. You don't need to run around town first."

He gripped her wrist and held her captive. She followed his lead and lowered herself on top of him. This time, she took control of the kiss, pulling strength from him, from their bond, to battle her morning. Shaye had to assume this was the reason the mate bond had been sealed the night before. To give them strength for whatever lies ahead.

Reluctantly, she pulled up, but he didn't let go of her wrist.

"I need to go."

"I'll be there. You won't see me, but I will be there."

"I know you will."

Nathan let go of her wrist and put his hand behind his head. His eyes followed her around the room while she dressed.

She looked over her shoulder as she left. Their eyes

locked long enough that he could pull her back if she let them. In order to follow through with this, she had to turn around and keep walking. The temptation of calling in sick like Nathan suggested was increasing.

Bear stood outside the house. He stuck his head under her hand and walked with her to her truck.

"Aren't you a gentleman." She scratched the back of his neck. "I suppose you'll be there too, huh?" He bobbed his head. "Be careful. And make sure Nathan is careful." His eyes locked with hers, identical orbs of Nathan's. He turned around and left her.

It was difficult to pull away, but she did it. The drive to her own home felt odd. It had only been a few days, but they stretched. Her home didn't quite feel right anymore. Something was missing or there was too much left untouched.

She could get lost in this analysis if she let herself. She could also get lost in thoughts of Nathan and their future together. Did this mean they needed to move in together? Would she need to sell her house? Would she want to live at Nathan's, or would he consider living in hers?

Shaye shook her head. She didn't have time for these thoughts.

Metaphorically pulling on her big girl pants, she made coffee, showered, dressed and picked up more coffee on her way into the office. Diana was already there and waiting.

"Right on time, Shaye. The files are there for you to print off. He asked that you try not to be late. I'm meeting with the Jennings' and also a new client this morning."

"All right." She smiled. *He's just a client. He's just a client. He's just a client.* The chant in her mind helped her to focus. This was work, her job. It had nothing to do with Nathan. She'd meet him. He'd sign the papers. And they would all move on as if there was no relation.

She worked on other messages while she waited for the papers to print. When it finished, she sorted through, sticking tabs in the places where they needed signatures or initials. She'd done this process enough it was second nature. She knew which pages required signatures.

Tucking the small pile into a manila envelope, she called back to her boss.

"All set. I'm heading out. I'll call you as soon as it's done."

"Perfect. Thank you, Shaye. We should celebrate with lunch."

"Sounds like a plan." It was the last thing Shaye wanted to do, but she wouldn't insult her boss.

He's just a client. This is just like any other day. She repeated herself for the ten-minute drive to Damien Marks' address. At the gate for the community, she had to give her name and reason for visiting to the two burly, bald guards. She was sure they were twins, but the facial hair on one was enough to make her wonder if maybe they were just a similar type. They nodded as soon as she said she was with the realtor. Opening the gate, they waved her through.

At the end of the subdivision was Damien's current home. It was a modern design with an off-angle roof. A dark colour scheme stood out amongst the lighter ones surrounding it. Not all houses were from the same cookie cutter mold, but it looked like a new, middle class, family subdivision. Shaye wondered what the reality of it was.

Damien stepped out on his front porch to meet her. She parked and stepped out of her truck. She had to pull in a breath to collect herself. A sharp heat pierced her and she knew it came from a set of eyes from somewhere in the distance. Nathan. He was here. She was safe. A small part of the tight ball in her gut unfurled and helped her relax. It added to the strength she gathered from Nathan before she left.

Straightening her shoulders, she walked up to the front of the house.

"Damien Marks? I'm Shaye Tierney, Diana's assistant."

"Nice to meet you, Miss Tierney." Shaye had to catch her breath before it left her body. His voice. There was a strong resemblance to Nathan's. There were similarities in their looks. But Nathan's voice was a part of her soul.

"Nice to meet you, too. I have all the paperwork we need. Should we get started?"

"Of course." He waved her ahead of him inside the house. "Please excuse my guests. Some of them were unexpected this morning." Inside his living room stood three other men, Zachary being one of them.

"That's not a problem." She smiled lightly.

"My apologies, Austin, but your business will have to wait until I'm finished with Miss Tierney."

"I can wait," said Zachary. Shaye held back her frown. Damien called him Austin. She made a mental note to demand at least some answers from him. She understood he didn't say much, like Nathan, but she put her trust in him, told Nathan she trusted him. He owed her at least a little information after this.

"You'll have to." Damien's face was cold as he stared at Zachary, but he quickly covered it with a smile as he gestured her ahead of him into the kitchen. She took the envelope from her bag and pulled out the papers.

"Everything is straight forward."

"Can I offer you something to drink?" He stopped at the island and pulled out a stool for her.

"No, thank you. I've had more than enough coffee this morning." She started giving quick summaries of each page, her familiar speeches calming her nerves. When she'd come to a place he needed to sign or initial, she quickly explained why and waited for him to do it before moving on. They went through each page twice, providing a signed copy for both him and them.

The familiar process went smooth and gave her hope there was nothing to worry about. When they reached the final page, she flipped them over onto their respective piles and smiled up at him.

"Congratulations, Mr. Marks. You just sold your house."

"Thank you. It's a relief to be rid of it." Any other client and Shaye would latch onto that and make conversation, building a connection with the client to produce recommendations and repeat business. Not this time. She gave him a sympathetic smile and straightened the contracts, tucking one back in the envelope and leaving the other on the counter.

"If we need anything further, we'll be sure to call." Shaye held out her hand and hoped she hid her shiver when he shook it.

"Pleasure doing business." He let her precede him from the kitchen. All three men in the living room stared at her as she walked by. She tried not to flinch or cringe under their scrutiny, but wasn't sure if she was successful. One flashed a grin before she turned away from them. "Have a lovely day, Miss Tierney."

"You as well, Mr. Marks."

She walked to her truck with her head still held high. Her body shook with the air she held in. She drove from the compound, nodding at the guards. When she was far enough away, she pulled over to the side of the road and let out a long breath. Her hands trembled on the steering wheel.

She looked up and in the trees along the road she saw a quick flash of brown eyes. She was safe. Everything went fine. There had been nothing to worry about.

Her mate was near.

SHAYE'S TREMORS rippled through Nathan's muscles as if they were his own. It killed him that he couldn't go to her. The road was too busy to allow for a grizzly to be seen. He had to watch while she gathered herself together and pulled back out into sparse traffic. He and Bear raced back to his place so he could make his own appearance at work. It would be hard to keep himself away from her.

The morning still held a cooler temperature, but the sun was bright. It wouldn't be long and the day would become a hot one. And Nathan did not want to be covered in fur for it.

He shifted outside of his house and set his hand on Bear's head before going inside. He froze before opening the door. The sound of an engine and the scent of a wolf carried itself up the lane. A motorcycle.

Nathan grabbed his pants from inside the door and slid them on, then leaned against the railing while Zachary got off his bike.

"Shaye was pretty shaken up. Anything happen?" Nathan crossed his arms and stared down the steps at the wolf shifter in leather.

"Nothing. But Damien wasn't the only one there. While he has no reason to harm Shaye, one of the others seemed to take an interest. When he realized I was still in the room, Damien dismissed me and told me to come back this afternoon. You need to keep an eye on her."

"An interest for what?" Nathan's insides crawled.

Keeping an eye on her wouldn't be enough. He wanted to hide her. Nathan knew several places they would never find them.

"I don't know. He's involved in a lot of shit. If Damien himself or anyone new starts sniffing around her, get her out of here." Zachary turned to leave.

"You going to tell me anything else?" Nathan called after him. "Like how you know Damien Marks and why he'll welcome you into his home?" Nathan had already been in the woods when Zachary had pulled up to his house.

"It's personal." He spoke over his shoulder.

"No shit. It's all personal."

"I'm trying to find..." He ground the words through his teeth then clamped his mouth shut, cutting himself off. He growled and kept walking to his bike. He kept his eyes away from Nathan as he put his helmet on.

Nathan wasn't okay with Zachary. Until he told him, at least him, about his connection to Damien, Nathan wouldn't trust him. Did he believe Zachary meant harm? No. He wouldn't warn Nathan about danger to Shaye if he did.

Life had been simpler when Nathan kept to himself and didn't care about other's secrets.

CHAPTER 18

Shaye had relaxed her guard. For days, there had been no calls from Damien Marks regarding the sale of his house and everything was going through.

She recognized the struggle still within Nathan for his search for answers, but he was pushing past it, ready to move on. He didn't want to put Shaye at risk like his mother. She had to admit, she was curious for answers. If there was a way to find out without asking Damien, she would do it. Just to put him at peace. But Shaye wouldn't go against him. Not now.

She convinced him to stay with her at her place for a while. They had yet to talk about what happened the night before her meeting with Damien. They sealed the mating bond. Their relationship skipped a few steps and talking about them now made little sense, except she wasn't sure if they were supposed to move in together, whose house they'd live in, if a wedding even mattered at this point, not that Nathan had asked her.

Now that things had calmed, she returned her friends' many messages and invited them over for dinner. Nathan raised his brow when she told him, but then nodded and went along with it.

Their evening started awkward. Her friends had things they wanted to say, but refused to. Once they relaxed, their focus shifted from her to Nathan. She almost sympathized, but now that they were permanently together, they would have to get used to each other. She'd let them figure it out on their own.

"So, you work at the lumber yard?" Chase asked.

"Yup."

"Are you from Alder Ridge?" Jenna asked.

"Yup."

They all sat in her living room, Nathan beside her on the couch and his arm resting across the back. Chase sat beside her and Jenna and Jerry in the chair together. Shaye felt a spike of amusement and realized it came from Nathan.

"Do you go camping? We all love camping, especially Shaye. You must, because she wouldn't be this serious with someone who didn't." Jenna was trying to taunt him into telling more and revealing more of their relationship. Shaye hadn't had much time to tell them how serious the relation-ship was, but they seemed to gather that on their own.

Nathan pursed his lips, giving the question some thought. "I don't really need to camp."

"Well, no one *needs* to go camping," said Jerry.

"No, but I already live in the woods near the lake. Your camping life is my life."

"No wonder Shaye has been spending so much time at your place." Jenna moved to the floor in front of Jerry. "Have you really been that busy at work lately, Shaye?"

"Yes. Back-to-back viewings and a couple sales. My boss is thrilled and I'm exhausted." They stopped pestering Nathan since he wasn't giving them any real answers, anyway. But neither did they treat Shaye the same as usual. There was a residual worry. Thanks to her new senses, she smelled it in each of them. All their worry had created a wound in their friendship and now the distance between them was noticeable. They were pulling away from her. Shaye couldn't decide how she felt about that.

Tonight had been an opportunity to reconnect, but it didn't work. She dreaded the idea, but maybe she would have to leave Nathan out of it. Spend time with them on her own, or at least Jenna.

"So, when is the next camping trip?" Chase nudged her arm. She looked over and he had his brows raised, waiting. Shaye was always the one to plan the trips. She planned them and her friends followed along so she wasn't alone. But this summer differed greatly from others.

"I haven't planned one." Three shocked faces stared back at her. She shrugged. "Sorry, guys." But their shock turned to frowns and all of them directed at Nathan as if this was a horrible thing and all his fault. "And on that note, I'm ready to call it a night." She stood and waited for them to follow.

One by one, they did.

"Let's do lunch tomorrow, Jenna," Shaye said to her at the door. This was her attempt to salvage their friendship. One on one time with Jenna might work and was her last hope. Jenna nodded, but didn't have time to respond as Jerry urged her out the door.

She shut the door and turned to Nathan. He held up his finger to keep her quiet, then pointed to the door. Shaye took a deep breath and tried to pull on her senses. She heard their faint voices and tried to make them out. She stepped closer to the door.

"...bad news."

"Jenna, you need to talk some sense into her tomorrow. You're the only one she'll listen to."

"I'm not sure why you think that, but I'll try. I'm not ready to call her a lost cause." The voices faded away, and she looked at Nathan.

"I missed the first half."

"They don't like me. They think I'm controlling you and that I'm bad news."

"That's all bullshit."

"You can't make them like me, sweetness."

"They aren't even trying, but neither are you."

Nathan shrugged.

Suddenly, his body tensed. Shaye saw a clear physical change. His nostrils flared, and he stood.

"I know this house." The masculine voice came from outside the door. She recognized it. Shaye clenched her hands into fists when they shook with the knock at the door.

Nathan didn't want her to answer the door, and neither did she, but they both heard more footsteps.

Shaye reached for the door, opening it slowly. She pretended recognition and opened it a little further. Not enough to be inviting, but enough not to be rude.

"Mr. Marks. Is there something I can help you with?"

"I'm sorry to bother you at home, but your name sounded familiar to me, and I couldn't get it out of my mind." Even Shaye could detect the lie. He only put the connection together just now. "I also had some questions about the sale." Another lie. She didn't need extra senses to detect that one.

"If you'll come into the office in the morning, I'd be happy to help with any questions you have." She plastered on her professional smile and had a firm grip on her door.

He ignored her dismissal and stepped closer, his hand pushing her door open.

"I believe I knew your father." He frowned and looked around the house. "We were friends growing up." He continued to look until his eye landed on Nathan.

"Really? That's very interesting."

"I'm interrupting company. This won't take long." He was talking to Shaye, but he focused on Nathan. Without another choice, and because the distance bothered her, she shut the door and moved to stand beside Nathan.

"Of course. What questions did you have?"

"You look familiar. Have we met?" he asked Nathan.

"No, we haven't."

The silence stretched.

"Mr. Marks? Your questions?"

His lips twitched. "My colleagues are the ones with questions." His eyes never left Nathan as the other two men came in through her front door. "You know, this is an interesting turn of events. I thought you were dead, son."

Shaye filled with her own fear and Nathan's rage. The threat hadn't passed at all. It knocked on her front door.

"Funny, I thought the same thing of you." Pretending wouldn't get them anywhere and only delay the inevitable. Nathan felt his teeth sharpen, but he needed to keep himself under control. As long as the two men that just entered didn't lay their hands on Shaye, he could. His problem would be guns. He was strong and he was fast, but he couldn't stop all three with guns. Auntie did it, though.

"We're all going to go for a little drive." He smiled, not a nice one. Everything that wasn't on his face reflected in his eyes. Nathan was hard pressed to read his emotions past his own anger. "I want to get to know my long-lost son. Then I'm afraid we must go back to my place. There's someone waiting to meet Miss Tierney." His immoral expression turned somber and he gestured for the two men to step forward. "I'm sorry to do this to my best friend's daughter, but such is life."

One reached for Shaye. "Don't touch her." His eyes widened at the sound of Nathan's voice. He didn't stop reaching for Shaye, but he moved slower.

"None of that. I'm sure you're aware of what I'm capable. I suggest you both come along nicely to avoid a fight."

Nathan looked over his shoulders then back at Damien. Inhaling, he caught the scent of metal, the guns they had beneath their jackets. The risk was too high. He grabbed Shaye and moved her in front of him, away from the other men and started walking them to the door. Once outside, one man led them to the waiting car, and the other walked behind them. Damien took his time looking around Shaye's house before following, shutting her door behind him. One last glance at the door and he turned and got in the front passenger seat of the car. It was a large sedan, but a tight fit just the same. Damien's men weren't small and Nathan himself took up half the back, pushing Shaye into the car door.

"Nathan." Damien turned in his seat. He spoke his name slowly, as if it were just as odd for him to say it as it was for Nathan to hear it. "Where do you live? I looked for you for years, but no one ever found a little boy, dead or alive."

Nathan gave him his address. He would happily have the three men on his property. "I have to ask. Why did you look for me?"

"You're my son. Why wouldn't I look for you?"

"Maybe I would understand if I knew what happened."

"That's a story for another time," he said grimly and turned back around, closing off the past.

The driver drove them straight to Nathan's.

"How convenient of you to live so isolated." Nathan didn't like his underlying message and had trouble deciphering his plan. They all got out of the car. "Walk with me, son." The two men flanked Shaye while Damien pulled at Nathan's elbow. "Calm down, boy. No one is hurting anyone unless I say so and it won't be your girl."

What Damien didn't understand, and what made this so dangerous for him and his men, was that Shaye wasn't just his girl. She was his soul. Mated, bound, and sealed to a shifter.

Damien walked toward Nathan's house, and Nathan didn't have a choice but to follow. "I have a dilemma. A client has requested the pickup of a parcel." He turned his head over his shoulder, his eyes finding Shaye. "He takes a fancy from time to time." His eyes brightened, a new excitement as his attention turned. "But this request has led me to you, my long-lost son." He looked over his house. "Who doesn't seem to be doing so well."

"Looks can deceive," Nathan murmured.

"I suppose they can. Are they in this case?" Damien's eyes met his. He had to tilt his head back to give the appearance of matching his height. If Nathan hadn't become a shifter, he might be an inch or two shorter. But if he hadn't become a shifter, he would have died with his mother.

Nathan smelled Bear coming up toward the back of the house. He heard him skulking over the ground. Anticipation coiled.

"I can give you a better life. I could have years ago."

"I assume the price is I let you take Shaye."

"Unfortunately," Damien sighed, "my hands are tied. But she won't come to any harm in my care."

"How comforting. Why bring us out here?"

"I wanted to see where my son lives." He puffed out his chest as if he had a reason to be proud of the son he knew nothing about, didn't even know was alive until twenty minutes ago. "I also can't bring you along to the exchange of the parcel I'm to deliver. So, you'll be staying here with one of my men until I can come back for you. It's time we got caught up, don't you?"

"I don't. And your plan won't go at all how you think it will."

Damien laughed, thinking Nathan was bullshitting. "What do you think you're going to do, boy?" But Bear was already making his way through the trees to move in on the other two from behind. They were both ready for a bloody mess.

Nathan grinned and waited for Bear to get in position.

"If you're going to be stubborn, we'll just have to do this the hard way. I'm going to leave, but one of my friends here will stay with you until I get back."

Bear's roar echoed. Damien spun around to see what was happening, but Nathan grabbed his collar. He pulled his fist back and brought it forward the same time he pulled Damien back around. The sound was sickening, despite the satisfaction it gave him. With the strength Nathan possessed, Damien fell unconscious to the ground.

Nathan's attention moved to Shaye. She got herself out of the middle and tucked behind their car. One man was bleeding out on the ground, the thump of his pulse in Nathan's ear was fading fast. He wouldn't move again. The second man that had been stationed at Shaye's left was fumbling with his gun at his back. He didn't see Nathan stalking toward him while he stared down Bear.

He got his gun free, but not before Nathan reached him. As he was raising it to shoot, Nathan gripped his hand and squeezed, crushing the tiny bones inside. The gun dropped to the ground. The snapping and cracking was worse than the contact with Damien's face. When Nathan released him, he fell to his knees, but wasn't smart enough to give up. He tried to reach for the gun with his other hand and Bear lunged. His teeth sank into the man's neck and he shook his head. The man's neck snapped, and he fell to the ground.

"Shaye?" Nathan called. She stood from behind the car. She looked at the bloody men on the ground. Her hand covered her mouth, and she closed her eyes. Nathan rushed to her and pulled her against him. "I'm sorry, sweetness." He sighed. "This isn't over yet."

He tucked her against his side and walked her to the house.

"Go inside." He pushed her forward, and she took one step up the stairs and froze.

"No. I'm not leaving you to deal with this on your own." She turned around, her eyes wider than they needed to be. Lifting her chin, she looked at Nathan, avoiding everything around them. He couldn't be more proud of her strength and willingness to stand by his side.

"Okay. But go take a few minutes, whatever you need. This won't be quick."

She gave him a shaky nod and went inside. He waited until she left before he turned to Bear.

"Any idea where Auntie hid the bodies when she found me?" Bear shook his head. "Guess we're on our own. But first I want to deal with him." He turned his glare on Damien. Nathan would get his answers after all.

SHAYE SAT down in a chair and slowly rocked back and forth while taking in deep breaths. She would not wimp out on Nathan. She was his mate, and she would be by his side. But there had been so much blood. And the sounds. Every single crunch, snap, gush, growl, and moan had scraped the inside of her ear. Her senses had been firing signals since Damien first knocked on her door. All of it overwhelmed her. Nathan was right to send her inside to recover.

She knew the death of Damien Marks was coming. He wouldn't be walking out of these woods, just like his two henchmen. Shaye didn't feel bad about that. She hoped Nathan learned what happened all those years ago, but she doubted it would make a difference in today's outcome.

When Damien had pulled Nathan away from her, a piece of her insides had cracked under the pressure. With them separated, they could have hurt either of them and she knew they would have if given a reason. But then she'd sensed Bear. She'd tracked him through the woods. The odds had turned, but the last thing she had wanted was for Bear to get hurt too.

She closed her eyes and listened to him move around the back of the car. When he paused and his claws dug into the ground, Shaye launched herself at the guys on her left. Behind her, she'd heard the vile sounds of Bear's attack. The man on her left moved with her, throwing her to the side, but on her way down she hooked her ankles around one foot, pulling his leg out from under him. He lost his balance and his grip.

She felt awful as she had crawled and hid behind the car. Some mate she was. But at least she'd distracted him long enough for Bear and Nathan to finish. Peeking over the side, she had seen both closing the distance.

There had been a strong stench of fresh fear. She'd recognized the scent because she smelled it on herself in the car ride here. But it hadn't been hers. It had belonged to the man fumbling for a gun that never got it raised before his throat had been ripped out by a beast.

Somehow reliving the scene in her head helped her move past it now. It wasn't the blood and attacks she saw anymore. She'd seen evil get what it deserved.

Her legs still shaky, she stood, went to the bathroom to splash some water on her face. Drying it off, she took in one breath, then another, and with each one she took a step toward the door.

Stepping outside, she noticed the only body Nathan moved was Damien's, and he moved it in a way that when he woke, he would see the bloody and maimed bodies of his men. And he would see the animal that did it.

Shaye kept her eyes off the men and focused on Nathan. She stretched her senses. What she discovered inside him would scare even the most evil of men. There was no hope for Damien Marks.

CHAPTER 19

Nathan knew the moment Shaye stepped outside. But he didn't have the time to comfort her again. Damien was waking up.

He groaned and rolled his head. "That wasn't smart, son." Arrogance laced his groggy tone until he opened his eyes, recognizing the blood surrounding him.

"You sure about that? Cause I'm not."

He watched Damien's eyes widen further with each body he looked at until he saw Bear standing to the side of one of them.

"There's a bear." He uttered the animal name through his breath. Nathan didn't bother restraining him, allowing him to crawl away. His hands on the ground behind him, he scurried a few feet before he fell.

"Stop." Nathan's command snapped in the air and Damien's shock turned on him. He hadn't expected much out of Nathan when he figured out who he was. Nathan might not have money, a large home or family, but he had power. Power that for the first time made him proud. Not because he had the ability to wield it over the man cowering on the ground and not because of that man's fate, but because it gave him morals and the ability to protect. "How do you feel about catching up with your son now?"

"You're not scared of the bear?"

"No, but don't let that stop you. You should be terrified."

"What happened to my men?"

"What does it look like? Do you really need an explanation?"

Damien shook while he straightened. He lifted his chin with practiced bravado. "What do you want?"

"Answers."

"You should leave the past where it is." Disgust poured from his mouth.

"That's exactly what I was going to do. Until you came after Shaye and brought us here. So, how about I start with what I know and you can fill in the blanks."

"Or what?" challenged Damien.

Nathan tilted his head toward Bear. No more words were needed.

Damien's face hardened. His jaw clenched and his eyes narrowed. His look of bravery and power didn't fool Nathan. Putrid smell of terror filled Nathan's nose.

"I know that you got in with some dirty business, but straightened yourself out around the time you met my mother. The three of us lived in a big family home until I was almost two. I know you disappeared and my mother had reason to believe you were dead. I know three men found my mother and I in a shack two years later and killed her because she wouldn't tell them where you were. And I know you're the head of an illegal shipping company."

"Sounds like you have all the information you need."

"I want more. I want to know why you left and why she thought you were dead."

"I didn't leave. I was taken. I was good at what I did, and they didn't want to let me go. But they weren't the only ones who wanted to use me."

"Who are they?"

"Doesn't matter. Both organizations were demolished years ago. They grabbed me from the yard. They let out a gunshot to warn me. They would have killed you both if I hadn't cooperated. For a while they let everyone believe I was dead so I wouldn't get snatched by someone else and used against them. The other side figured it out and thought my wife would know where to find me. Why didn't they kill you too?"

"I escaped."

"A four-year-old?"

"Yup." Nathan crossed his arms. "You're free of them now. Why are you still doing it?"

"I like it. I always have. The only reason I got out was for your mother. The drugs, the sex, the money, I crave it all. I regret losing you both. But she knew who she married."

"That's all I needed to hear." Nathan started stripping his clothes. He considered shifting with them on, let the change tear them off, but it was a habit. And there was no need to destroy good clothes just for show.

"What are you doing?"

Bear walked around the back of Damien. Standing naked in front of him, the animal within reached upward toward freedom. He looked up at the house. Shaye stood stock still, her grip on the railing turning her knuckles white. "Shaye, go inside." She shook her head. "Now, Shaye. You don't want to see this."

"I don't, but I'm not leaving." Stubborn woman. Nathan

didn't want to do this in front of her. She wasn't trying to stop him. She was trying to be there for him. He understood, and it meant more to him than he could say, but he wouldn't let her watch.

"Go, Shaye. Please." Even his plea was a low growl. Shaye turned around and held her hand on the door, but she didn't open it. Fuck, he was a lucky bastard.

Nathan wasn't a murderer. Except for today. This day would stain his soul, but there wasn't any way around this. He couldn't leave Damien alive to come after him or Shaye again. Someone would step up in his place and evil would still have its hold in the world, but just not this particular evil.

Nathan shifted.

"What the fuck is happening?" Damien tried to brace himself to stand, but lost his footing, falling back to the ground.

The wind sagged sadly in the air a few feet away. It wasn't stopping him either. Covered in fur and his eyes flashing, he looked at the wind and threw out the question to the magic around him. Was this meant to be?

The wind parted and through it walked a woman. The same woman that had appeared at Asher's wedding. A ghost from the past. The winds had come from her or had been sent by her. Her long braid swayed over her shoulder with a breeze that wasn't there.

Sorrow bled from her eyes without a single tear. Her feelings, and he could sense them, mirrored his. She nodded her head once and closed her eyes in resignation.

Nathan moved before he analyzed further.

He charged. Damien's scream barely left his throat before Nathan clamped his jaws around it and twisted his head, snapping Damien's neck.

The threat was gone. His mate was safe.

SHAYE CRINGED, her hand over her mouth to hold in her cry. She wanted to turn around, but she froze, her skin chilled and her muscles iced. The hatred Nathan had for himself stabbed her in the back. A tear slipped down her cheek. He convinced himself he had to do it. And maybe he did, but it didn't make it easy on him.

Sudden awareness licked her spine and forced her to spin around. A grey wolf charged through the woods. Straight at Nathan, jaws covered in his father's blood. In the air in his path was the auburn wind with which Shaye was becoming familiar, but with the wind was a woman. Shaye's jaw went slack. She was transparent, not really there. And the wolf charged straight through her.

Her image distorted, but came back together to watch the animals. A puff of smoke appeared with the brown wind.

Shaye was in such awe that the snarling and snapping she had known was coming startled her. She turned back in time to see the wolf and Nathan rolling together in a ball before each regaining their balance. The grey wolf must be Zachary.

He charged at Nathan again. Bear tried to defend him, but the wolf was too quick. Shaye didn't know what to do. She didn't fear Zachary would hurt Nathan. It was two against one. But the bears could hurt Zachary. And he was mad enough not to stop.

More sounds rushed through the trees. Three more wolves, two white and one identical to Zachary. Smoke tackled Zachary while he fought to get past him, and the two white wolves stood between the bears and the grey wolves.

Asher shifted and looked at Nathan. He followed suit, but cringed as the change must have been painful with the teeth marks from Zachary. Smoke still struggled to control Zachary.

Shaye stood motionless on the steps with no way to help. Not with something that had Zachary in a violent fury. When Smoke had his leg pinned in his jaw, he finally shifted. Smoke released him.

"Why the fuck did you kill him? Do you have any idea what you've done?" Agony drenched Zachary's voice as he yelled across the yard. His emotions poured from him. If she felt it, then so could the other shifters.

"What are you talking about?" Nathan growled low.

"It was already impossible. You've made it worse." His fingers tore through his hair. His bare feet stomped on the ground, snapping twigs in his path.

"Made what worse, Zachary?" Asher turned to face him and Nathan stood beside Asher. With the shifters back in human form and two out of the three calm, Shaye walked down the stairs to join them. Slowly.

"Why did you fucking do it?" Zachary whirled on Nathan, his face brewing to a deep red. His eyes not his own, but the wolf's. Thin silvery smoke swirled around the dark pupils.

"I had to."

Shaye wrapped her hands around Nathan's wrist. He was hurting, and she hurt hearing the disgust coming from inside him.

"I'll never find her." Zachary spoke to the ground.

"Find who?" asked Nathan. Zachary didn't answer, lost in his own tortured mind.

His grey wind appeared in front of him and with it came the woman she saw earlier. Her lips moved, but Shaye couldn't hear her. Asher and Nathan leaned forward, but by the looks on their faces, they couldn't hear her either. The words were for Zachary only. Her eyes held the same sorrow Shaye saw in all of them.

After a moment, the woman slowly faded away and the smoky wind embraced Zachary while he shifted. He looked at Smoke, then started off into a run with Smoke behind him.

"You guys aren't going to stop him?"

"No." Nathan sighed. "He'll either come back or we'll go find him after he's had some time."

"You've changed." Asher turned a frown on Nathan.

"Yes, I have. More than even I'm aware." He cupped Shaye's chin and lifted her to look into her eyes. His were deep pools with so many emotions drowning in them. "Go inside. Shower, make tea, go to bed. Whatever you need to do. Thank you for not leaving me. But now I need to clean up and you need to take care of yourself until I'm able to do it for you."

"Okay," she whispered, her own breath warm on her lips. He swiped his thumb across her mouth before he released her. He gave her a little nudge to get her inside. She didn't want to leave him, but there wasn't anything she could do now. She would make herself strong to be here for him when he finished.

"I want to go after him." Asher took a step forward, his body tensing for a shift. Nathan grabbed his arm, surprised he needed true strength to stop him.

"Don't. I'll help you find him tomorrow, but give him some time." If they chased him, it would make things harder. And Nathan wanted to be there when Zachary finally talked. He couldn't go right now. Not with a pile of dead bodies to deal with.

"You saw the woman too, right?" Asher's gaze landed on the path Zachary and Smoke took.

"Yeah." She never left after she showed herself to him.

"Did you hear her?" he asked, turning his attention back to Nathan. Although, Asher's focus wasn't on him.

"Not everything. *Guide you* were the only words I heard." Nathan had strained to hear even that much.

"Same." Asher paused. "Who do you think she is?"

"A ghost from the past."

"She's more than that." Asher sounded ready for an argument. Nathan sensed his adrenaline and his need for a distraction to keep himself from following Zachary.

"I know it." He had a feeling her story would be revealed one day and in her own time. There was no point dwelling on it now. Especially when he had stuff to take care of. "I've got work to do."

"We'll help." Asher looked over at Kai, who nodded his head.

"You don't have to do that. This isn't your mess. You don't need to get involved in this." Nathan shouldered enough guilt.

"This is why I've brought us together." In a single moment, Asher's eyes flashed a bright blue and his height grew, displaying the alpha wolf he was. The leader.

"You brought us together to help each other bury bodies?" Nathan couldn't pass the opportunity. His lips twitched and something inside him caved when Asher's did too.

"Yeah, pretty much."

A friend. Nathan was building his first friendship.

IT WAS morning before Nathan stepped inside his house. His limbs were weighted enough his knuckles should be dragging on the ground. The bodies were gone. Deep into the mountains where only nature reigned. They'd feed the wildlife and their remains spread throughout as animals fight for scraps. The car was most likely a full pile of ash, hours outside of town. Nathan lit the seats, the brake fluid, and the trunk on fire. He watched it long enough to know it would burn. They almost put the bodies in it, but they didn't in case someone caught the fire before the care finished burning. He didn't want the bodies to ever be found.

Shaye was asleep on his couch. The sleeve of his t-shirt covered her shoulder while her arm held the blanket tight under her chin. Tissues littered the floor next to an empty mug. Her hair was away from her face in a frayed braid. Her skin looked so soft. He longed to touch it. But not with his hands. Not these hands.

He stalked to the shower with light steps and washed away the memories of the night along with the dirt and blood. The lake hadn't washed it all away, but it was enough for two white wolves to travel home.

Nathan stood under the heat until sensation returned. Careful footsteps sounded outside the bathroom door. He ducked his head for the water to hit his back and run down his neck, heating his spine. Shaye opened the door and stepped in. Nathan turned and pulled her into the spray, the urge to have her close overtook him.

"Nathan." Her soft voice soothed him, but he put his finger over her lips.

"I don't need to talk it out. It is what it is, and I wouldn't have done anything different. I got the answers I didn't think I would ever get. I avenged my mother and the life she didn't even have the chance to live. And I've kept you safe from him."

"What about his client who sent him after me?"

"We'll deal with him if he comes after you. The organization will be scrambling for a while."

Shaye heaved a sigh and leaned her cheek against his chest. Their hearts adjusted their rhythms until they beat in unison. The dual thumping increased and sent the blood heating through their bodies. It was dizzying to feel the sensations through Shaye and himself.

Her dazzled eyes lifted to his and her mouth fell open in an invitation he couldn't resist. He claimed her mouth and allowed his hands to do as they pleased, moving over her body as if he'd never get to touch her again. The reality of the night was he might not have. He owed that to Bear.

His mind cleared of everything except Shaye, except burying himself in her heat and getting lost. He lifted and put her back to the wall. Putting his forehead to hers, he thrust forward, her walls greedily wrapping around his cock. Their breath mingled in the steam of the room.

This wasn't frantic love making like every other time. This was pure need for both of them. They weren't trying to chase down pleasure created by the mate bond. Their own inner needs for the one they loved were dominating. This was the connection they had deep down, the ties that kept them together.

The water chilled with their slow pace, building to the peak. When she went over hers, her heat gently squeezing, his climax raced up his cock and spilled inside her. He stayed there and kept her pinned to the wall while he shut off the water.

"I love you, sweetness." He didn't have to say it. He knew she felt it, heard it echoing within her. Just as he heard it from her.

"I love you too." But hearing the words filled part of him with content.

Nathan dried them off in the bathroom and carried her to bed. He paused. He sent a quick text to her boss, then turned off her phone before crawling in behind her. Shaye needed rest as much as he did.

SHAYE WOKE with a start and reached for the nightstand to check her phone. The sun shining in the windows was too high in the sky for her to still be in bed. She grabbed her phone and pressed the bottom of the screen, but the screen stayed black.

"I turned it off." His sleep-heavy voice moaned.

"You did what?"

"Shaye, you aren't going into work today."

"You don't get to make that decision."

"I'm sorry, but I did exactly that. I sent a message to your boss first. Then shut your phone off so you could get rest and take the day to lie low."

Her fight left her. He was right. The last thing she wanted right now was to deal with work.

"Come back..." he stopped. "Never mind. We have company coming."

Shaye frowned and tried to listen. Her senses weren't what they'd been the night before, but she heard tires on the lane. Nathan got out of bed and put on a clean pair of jeans from his dresser and tossed her a t-shirt. They met Asher and Gwen at the front door. Nathan leaned against the frame and pulled Shaye against him, wrapping an arm possessively around her shoulders. His heat engulfed her back. A t-shirt wasn't enough clothing to meet company, but Shaye found she didn't have the energy to care. She rested her head against his chest and leaned into him.

Asher parked the truck. Gwen jumped out first and Asher took his time. His longer stride had him catching up to Gwen by the time she reached the bottom of the steps.

"You look like you're okay." Gwen tilted her head as her eyes travelled up and down Shaye.

"I am. Do you guys want to come in?"

"Sure." Gwen stepped forward, but Asher waited. Nathan didn't move from behind her either. Shaye turned her head to frown at Nathan.

"Yeah, come on in," he conceded. Shaye went to the bedroom to get dressed before following them all back to the kitchen.

"Any word from Zachary?" Nathan asked once Asher and Gwen had settled at the table.

"Not exactly. Smoke talked to Kai. He said they were leaving. But with or without Zachary, Smoke would be back. He's settled in with the pack and didn't want to leave it, but he had to follow him."

"And I saw him before they left, but he wouldn't tell me anything. He left his bike at our place." Gwen wouldn't meet their eyes as she spoke. She watched her fingers twist together in her lap. She'd told Shaye how concerned she was for Smoke and Zachary.

"Damien called him Austin." Shaye's thought felt ill

timed, but Zachary seemed to be a mystery to all of them and had a problem he was trying to deal with on his own.

"Zachary is his middle name, but we didn't know his first," said Gwen.

"Would he have given Damien his real name?" Shaye wouldn't have given a man like him any real personal information.

"Don't know. We don't know how he knew him." Asher leaned forward, his forearms on the edge of the table.

"Do you want to hunt him down?" asked Nathan.

"Smoke said not to. For now."

The events from the previous night weighed heavily on all of them. It was almost a physical thing Shaye could see. Silence blanketed the room until Gwen and Asher decided that with nothing they could do, they might as well go home. Try to pull their patience together to wait for the grey wolves to return.

After seeing them out, Shaye joined Nathan back in the kitchen.

He turned in his chair and beckoned her over to his lap. The pull between them was irresistible. They were tied together in so many ways. She was no longer mad at Fate for all of her little puzzle pieces and stepping stones in her life. Shaye might not like them, but Fate had her reasons.

It felt like they were only beginning with their relationship, but starting at a different point than what was normal. So much had changed. Her friends, her job, her views on her life. Shaye needed to take a step back.

"Nathan?"

"Yes?"

"I need a break. I need a change. My life isn't what I think it is anymore. Can we take a vacation?"

He grinned, and his muscles relaxed beneath hers. "I think that's exactly what we need to do."

Shaye wanted to push a large refresh button and see what everything looked like after. She was bound and tied to a new world and a new life. A wild and magical one with the bear she loved.

Everything else could wait for a little while. Zachary needed time. She and Nathan would create their foundation in the meantime and be stronger for it. And be ready when Fate brought the next obstacle.

Zachary went home to Hull Creek. Smoke refused to go with him. He understood Smoke was still hurt, but at least he knew why Zachary disappeared. For Holly. Only for Holly. But Zachary couldn't save her without him, without the other half of his soul by his side.

Smoke was the closest thing to a brother he had. It was rough growing up as unacceptable in both sides of his life. Not his parents. Never his parents. But the community, his teachers, his friends' parents, other wolves. They all looked down on him. In a small town, all it took was one bad decision. Though that didn't explain the wolves' opinion of him.

None of that mattered anymore. Zachary didn't care then, and he didn't care now.

What he did care about was earning Smoke's trust again.

Zachary packed light. He could only carry so much as a wolf. He made a promise to his parent's and to Holly's parents that he would find her, his surrogate little sister. They all believed it to be an empty promise. It wasn't. It took over two years to finally find a trail only to lose it with the death of Damien Marks. The one man with all the information.

But then the only piece of information he needed came from a ghost. An address with a warning that it wouldn't be easy to get her out.

Zachary wasn't going to do this without Smoke. They'd already spent too much time apart. He'd gotten the call from his mother that Holly was missing. A few days had passed and they discovered Holly had been taken, but the police didn't know by who or why. Zachary had gone into a rage, only thinking about finding Holly, thinking he didn't have even a minute to lose. He'd left Hull Creek and picked up the trail the police had lost, leaving Smoke behind. By the time Zachary had returned defeated from finding dead ends, Smoke was gone. A fresh rage overtook him and he began a frantic search for Smoke with no luck, until he smelled Gwen at *Bucky's Cafe* when she came searching for him in Hull Creek.

Asher and Gwen had found Smoke, or rather Smoke had found them. Zachary owed them. Smoke might have gone too far, his mind lost, if it weren't Gwen, Asher, and Kai, Asher's wolf.

Zachary locked up his apartment, two rooms above a mechanic's garage, and ran down the outside stairs to his motorcycle. He drove from Hull Creek back to Alder Ridge, arriving in the middle of the night. He parked in Asher's driveway. Saying a silent farewell, and promise that he'd be back, to his bike, he darted into the woods. He ran full force until he reached Kai's territory, Smoke's new home.

Smoke and Kai met him in the centre of their territory. Patches of Kai's fur were stained, still showing evidence from what happened at Nathan's.

Come with me, Smoke. Please. He knew he was begging. There was nothing left for him to say or do to earn Smoke's trust and respect.

Smoke didn't answer.

I don't want to leave you again. If it weren't Holly, I wouldn't. I couldn't. Smoke, I need you by my side this time. I panicked before. I'm not panicking anymore.

Jagged huffs of hot air pushed out of Smoke's snout and Zachary saw his claws twitch and dig into the ground. Smoke looked at Kai.

You should go with him. You'll regret it if you don't. It surprised Zachary that Kai agreed with him. He held his breath, waiting for Smoke's response.

Fine. I'll go.

Thank you, Smoke, my brother. Zachary closed the distance and touched his head to Smoke's. Both wolves closed their eyes, but it was only seconds before Smoke grunted and pushed his head off. *I need to grab my bag off my bike.*

Zachary started through the trees, but turned when he realized Smoke wasn't following. He looked back and saw Smoke and Kai touching heads. Echoes of their conversation tickled his ears. They stepped back and gave nods of respect. A stab of guilt hit Zachary. He was taking Smoke away from his home. His home may have been with Zachary, a lonely home, at one time, but not anymore. It didn't matter if Zachary managed to repair the damage with Smoke, Smoke would never leave this home.

Smoke caught up and they ran back to Asher's. Emerging from the trees, they skidded to a halt when they saw Gwen standing next to Zachary's bike.

"What are you two doing?"

Zachary stood still. He didn't want their help. None of them deserved to get involved in this.

Are you going to shift and answer her? Smoke tilted his head and snapped at Zachary.

No. I'm not.

Smoke snarled and lunged at Zachary's throat. Zachary twisted in time to block him. *Tell her!*

I can't! Zachary returned Smoke's snarl. *I couldn't take it if any of them got hurt because of me, because of whatever it is I'd be dragging them into. I don't even know what I'm walking into.*

Heaving with anger, Smoke turned away from him and walked to Gwen. He leaned his head against her stomach and closed his eyes. Frowning, Gwen put both hands on his head and held him close.

"You're leaving." Her tears were in her voice rather than her eyes. Zachary liked Gwen so the hurt from her disappointment wasn't a shock.

He gripped the bag in his jaw and pulled it off his bike.

We need to go, Smoke. Before Asher comes. He'll try to stop us.

Maybe he should stop us. Smoke still hadn't pulled away from Gwen.

I don't want them hurt. And I know you don't either.

Smoke sighed and pulled away, his eyes cast to the ground. Zachary nodded at Gwen then turned to run through the trees. He paused when Asher appeared in his door with a towel wrapped around his waist. He shook his head, silently asking them not to leave. Zachary couldn't do as he asked.

The trip wasn't a short one, but he wanted to cover as much ground as possible, increasing the distance from those who Smoke cared about most. Even Zachary was beginning to care about them.

We'll come back. I promise.

Smoke grunted and kept pace. Zachary's heart sank as another string from their connection snapped. His promise didn't mean much to Smoke anymore.

Join my newsletter to receive special content, the most up to date information on releases, and special promotions.
http://bit.ly/sarahurquhart

Also, visit my website at...
http://www.authorsarahurquhart.com
... to see my full book list.

Keep reading for an excerpt from **Silver Chains, Wounded Winds Book Three.**

http://www.books2read.com/woundedwinds3

SILVER CHAINS

Zachary missed his motorcycle. Driving around this shit hole city in the same damn car as everyone else grated on his nerves. He drove the simple, small, grey SUV that appeared around every corner. He didn't want to stand out, and that was exactly what his motorcycle would do. And he hated it.

He'd been scouting out the address the woman, ghost, spirit, other being, whatever the hell she was, gave him. And he found nothing other than a building of offices. Each floor housed a different business. Insurance broker, realty agency, lawyer offices, and a public relations agency. When researching them, Zachary found well-built websites and contact information, but not much marketing. His attempts to contact each of them, posing as potential clients, only garnered recorded responses or automated messages. Access to the building was only granted with a passkey and no windows could open, were reinforced, and tinted.

The entire building was a front for something. But Zachary still didn't know what. The woman only gave him an address and a reassurance that Holly was mostly unharmed. *Mostly unharmed.* Those words ate at him with each day that passed, and he still hadn't found her. No sign whatsoever. But he'd been observing the patterns of the building.

Maybe she'd been wrong. If so, this had been a fucking waste of time. Time that he could have really used to find her.

Zachary drove to the campsite outside of town. He camped to make it easier to shift and to stay near Smoke, and he chose the side of town closest to where Holly was being held. Smoke stayed near the camp, but out of sight of the other campers. Zachary often went for *hikes* to shift and spend time with Smoke.

Zachary healed with Smoke by his side every day, but it wasn't the same for his wolf brother. Smoke still hurt from being abandoned by Zachary, even if that hadn't been his intention. Searching for Holly alone had been foolish and useless. And it had torn the two of them apart.

He arrived at camp and went in search of Smoke. Evening settled over the sky and the scent of the air changed with the coming of night. Campers were gathering around their fires, no longer wandering the trails. A couple hundred metres on the trail, Zachary veered off. He found the area Smoke claimed as a temporary territory. He moved around when he had to due to campers coming too close. Smoke hated it and told Zachary each day how much he missed Kai's pack. Zachary's jealousy grew, but he wasn't in the position to do anything. He had lost the right to feel this way.

Zachary ditched his clothes and hid them in a hole under a rock. A rock too heavy for most humans to move, but easy enough for a shifter. He shifted, the process beginning in his mind, then moved to his soul, pushing an ache through his body as each bone changed its position. Time as a wolf had been Zachary's escape from life while growing up. But it also came with its own challenges. He hadn't been treated any better by other wolves than he had by other humans.

He landed on the ground as the final waves of magic washed over him. Smoke emerged, dinner hanging from his jaws. He dropped the grouse in front of Zachary.

Still nothing? Smoke asked. They'd been there for almost three weeks and Zachary had yet to find a way into that building or confirm Holly was inside. Even a shifter's sense of smell couldn't penetrate the walls.

Nothing. Zachary had reached a dead end. So much rage and frustration filled his gut, but he refused to let it out. Because of Smoke. But some of Zachary's rage was directed at the death of Damien Marks. Zachary might have an address, but without Damien, he couldn't get inside.

How long are we going to stay here?

Smoke, if you want to go back to Kai's pack, then go. I can't force you to stay with me. Zachary snapped, some of his frustration leaking out. His tone filled with bitterness.

That isn't it. I'm with you. Smoke still hadn't laid down to eat the grouse. Zachary felt the strength of Smoke's eyes on him. *What you're doing isn't working. We need a different angle.*

You don't want to leave? Zachary had been sure he'd been miserable with him.

Smoke looked away and a long huff came out his nose. *I'm still hurt and I know I shouldn't be. Not when I know how important Holly is to you. But it hurts just as much to be away from you. I'm with you. Brother.* Zachary's breath lurched as the word he'd needed most came from Smoke. Brother.

Maybe I need to get in touch with some contacts I'd rather avoid. See who took the place of Damien. It was the last thing he wanted to do.

Over the past month, Zachary had filled Smoke in on what he'd been doing for two years, how he'd finally found a trail and wormed his way into their circle enough to gain some trust. He'd been disgusted with himself anytime he stood next to Damien or anyone else inside that organization.

And Zachary had filled with remorse as Smoke told him of what he'd done for two years. Alone. Angry. Vicious. He'd become a whole different wolf. Zachary recognized how much he'd changed. And, Zachary thought, he had too.

I want to try for a little longer before contacting that group again. He hoped it never came to that.

Okay. After a firm nod, Smoke lay down to eat. Zachary followed, grateful to have his brother back, but the rift still needed to heal.

Ezaray had lost count of the days after two years had passed. Her hope of ever escaping disappeared a long time ago. The only thing that kept her going was she knew this could be worse. Women were usually kidnapped for one purpose, and for the women here, that wasn't it. The women here needed to be kept healthy. She guessed they should be thankful for small miracles. They staffed the building with its own doctor and security. They let anyone caught treating the captives with anything worse than a shove *go*. All the women knew what they meant when they said *let go*. Let go meant someone was fired, but not here. Killed. They killed violators to let them go. Ezaray wasn't naïve. Not all women were in good standing here. If one lost too many times in a row, they disposed of them.

They had taken her and Holly on Holly's birthday. Holly had sensed them closing in, but she was too late. Ezaray knew she still blames herself for it every day, even though she stopped telling her.

Turning twenty had felt like such a big deal. Her life unfolding, and she'd been excited to dig in. Beginning a new job where she could grow and learn.

All that had happened. Just not the way she'd expected it would.

They hadn't gone to a club to drink, dance, and celebrate, but they had gone to the pub and stayed well into the night on their patio ordering appetizers and drinks. There had been four of them, Ezaray, Holly, and two other friends from high school. She didn't know what happened to them. They never saw them here. She grieved for her friends with the only assumption they had for what happened to them. But not long, and not often. There hadn't been the time when they worried about their own future.

Her handler kept her busy. For now, she and Holly had the same handler, but handlers changed. And when they did, they would set Ezaray against her best friend. It had happened before and would happen again. They traded and sold the women between handlers often. All part of their business.

The handlers watched for when they let each other win so as not to put their friend's life in danger, but rarely did they catch Holly pulling back. But that was because they didn't know Holly's true strength. She never allowed herself to show it. Holly had saved it for an escape someday, when she had still thought an escape was possible. To everyone else, Holly still seemed optimistic. Ezaray expected she put on an act, holding onto her hope solely to give to the other women and not for herself. That would be a Holly-like thing to do.

"Tallon, you fight tonight." Her handler appeared in their doorway, bedrooms disguised as offices. Gerard Young wasn't the worst handler in the company, but he only cared about the money and had no problem saying whatever to scare the shit out of Ezaray, Holly, or whoever else he controlled. The words worked on some of the newer girls.

"I thought Seely was fighting tonight." Ezaray learned to keep her voice small, compliant.

"She didn't make it." Gerard held a gravely joy in his one-sided sneer and a delightful spark in his eye. Ezaray refused to react, refused to swallow or allow her lips to twitch or her nostrils to flare, refused to allow Gerard to see a single tear fall with fear shining in the drop. She gave no reason for any handler to think her weak. She stared into his evil eyes for only a moment before she sat on her bed and pulled out her gear to prepare for the fight.

Gerard walked away, his slow footsteps fading. Holly emerged from the corner.

"Poor Kate." Her throat lodged on Kate's name. Kate had been trying hard for a long time, but as the days passed, her energy, her will to stay alive wavered. She'd lost her last fight. Holly knelt on the floor in front of Ezaray and helped her prepare. "Kate was supposed to fight Maggie tonight. Maggie's good, Zee." She didn't speak with awe of Maggie's skills, but fear that Ezaray's didn't match hers.

"I'll be fine, Holly." Her grief over Kate kept her voice flat. Empty words were the norm when trying to encourage Holly. They both knew the truth of their situation. She kept the words, but let go of the hope.

Holly and Ezaray were two of the best fighters in the company, but so was Maggie.

In her shorts and sports bra and with her hands wrapped, Ezaray ran through some warm-ups and drills with Holly while waiting for Gerard to tell her it was time to go.

The rain would provide an excuse. As long as Zachary's acting skills were up to par. He stalked the alleys, waiting for the *well-dressed men* to enter the building. The apparent business hours were erratic. Zachary tracked movement for a pattern, but the people coming and going weren't consistent. He familiarized himself with recurring scents and features. The pattern may not be consistent, but the clientele was.

He'd studied each man that walked into the building for the past two weeks. He knew who the difficult targets would be by their arrogant struts and high chins. And he recognized the weak and new clients by how their eyes searched the area as they approached the building and again before they opened the door. Their gait was slower than others, and their posture didn't carry the straight sharpness that increased their height and changed the air surrounding them. These were the easy targets, the ones he intended to con.

Zachary had gone shopping earlier in the day, to dress to match others. Button-up dress shirts and slacks. Sweaters and sweater vests adorned some older patrons, but Zachary would never touch them. The dress code of business casual matched the businesses labelled in white decals on the glass of the front door.

He yanked off the tag on the sleeve of the navy blue button-up shirt and rolled up the cuffs. Sinking his body against the building across the street to hide himself in shadows, he watched the door and the men that approached, waiting for the right moment, the right target.

And there he was. Short, young, and grew up with money and privilege. He wore tailored clothes, but he'd yet to grow into the broader shoulders of his frame. He walked with self assurance until he got closer to the building. His steps faltered and his head turned from side to side with the smallest movements.

The street emptied, the crowd entering slowed for the moment. Zachary dashed from the alley, the rain sticking his shirt to his chest and back.

The grey wind quickly blew through the street as he crossed. He watched it disappear, knowing it meant something important, but he refused to get distracted.

"Hold the door!" he boomed through the rain the moment the guy ran his passkey over the box outside the door. Zachary grabbed the frame above his head and shook out his hair. In his other hand he held a blank white card. It did nothing and didn't hold the same luster as the passkeys he'd seen people use, but in the dimness of the rainy evening, it passed inspection for any cameras and the young guy in front of him.

Zachary glared down at him and watched him visibly swallow. He took one step to face Zachary.

"In." He gestured with his hand enough that the guy noticed the white card between his fingers. The guy moved and Zachary followed, keeping his eyes forward and using his sense of smell to track his surroundings.

The inside looked like any other high-end business. Plush waiting areas sat on each side of the door, their fabric without a single dent, rip or stain. A man in his sixties with a blue security uniform sat behind the main desk staring at computer monitors. Zachary wondered if his job was just for show. A place running an illegal business should have better security than him.

And they did.

That security stood in the form of a man larger than Zachary next to the elevators at the end of the lobby. He blocked one boarded up elevator entrance. The other elevator had the same electronic box on the outside to call it.

Zachary stayed behind the smaller man — kid, he was barely a man — and kept his card in his hand. The box beeped as the kid ran his key over it. The security guy eyed him, then Zachary. Zachary returned his glare and nodded, lifting his hand so he saw his card. The guy hesitated, but the elevator opened and Zachary moved in beside the kid before he could say anything. He'd gotten lucky with his timing. Getting in shouldn't have been that easy.

The elevator had one direction — down. He'd be trapped underground. His muscles tensed as he prepared himself the best he could. The kid watched Zachary with the side of his eye. He quickly turned his head away when Zachary glared at him. Zachary's lips twitched as he smelled fear spike for a moment from the kid. He was easy to intimidate. The problem was, even Zachary was feeling a bit intimidated by his situation. There'd be no way out if he was caught as soon as those doors opened.

Zachary's senses ran wild when the doors opened. He stepped out of the elevator without anyone stopping him. At first glance, the room looked to be a gentlemen's club. Cigar smoke floated around the air. Glass tumblers of amber liquid were in the hands of most of the men. A shiny, dark stained, wooden bar ran along one entire wall with five male bartenders behind it. Security guards similar to the one on the floor above roamed. Booths, tall tables, and end tables with plush furniture circled the room. But what stood out amongst it all, out of place for a gentleman's club, was the fighting ring in the centre.

Whatever he just walked into started a sickness in his gut that tried to eat its way out with a burning sensation.

The kid walked off, joining a group his own age that greeted him with cheers. Zachary ambled over to the bar, watching the other customers to see what they required when ordering a drink. Simple cash. Green twenties passed from the customers to the bartender.

A lanky bartender, white shirt, black vest, stood across from him with a raised brow.

"Whiskey." Zachary pulled out a twenty he had tucked beside his wallet and passed it over. Seconds later, the bartender set his glass in front of him and moved on to the next guy.

Two chairs and a small table sat empty in a darker alcove. Zachary made his way over and sat to observe the room. Without knowing the purpose of this place, he didn't want to talk to anyone and make it known he didn't belong.

The scents were strong and plenty. Several flavours of cigars and cologne mingled together. Strong amber alcohols filled most glasses. And the distinct scent of cash wafted here and there. Men of all ages, but all wealthy, stood in groups, a few meandering with social delight.

After half an hour, a clearing of a throat echoed through unseen speakers. Attention turned toward the ring. A man dressed in a black suit stood in the centre, smiling at the room, his white teeth showing beneath his shaped, dark facial hair. A ponytail pulled his hair tightly away from his face.

"Welcome, gentlemen." He held a microphone in one hand. The club took up the entire basement space of the building. "Tonight's event promises to be a good one. Our girls will come around shortly to collect your bets. A reminder, the minimum bet is five thousand dollars. If you're new or have yet to get to know some of our girls, do so this evening. Find your favourite and invest in their future." Excitement rose in his voice as he spread his arm outward to encompass the club. His eyes were wide and focused above a grin meant to seduce the men to spend their money.

Excited faces donned many of them, and their eyes often looked toward the back of the room. Zachary kept himself seated. After ten minutes, an elevator dinged in the distance and the atmosphere of the murmurs changed.

Female scents filtered through the crowd. Their anxiety-tinged aromas soured his nose. The well-groomed centre man implied the girls were here of their own free will, choosing this to make a life for themselves. They weren't and every person in this room knew it.

The men parted, giving Zachary glimpses of the girls making their way through the crowd individually. All wearing short spandex shorts and sports bras and carrying tablets with an electronic tap to record bets and accept money. A redhead waded through the men, but she wasn't carrying a tablet like the rest. Fabric wrapped her hands, as if ready for a boxing match. The fighting ring was for the girls. If there was one fighter, then there was another floating through the crowd.

Zachary had to force his breathing to create a steady pace when his body would rather rush air in and out of him like the quick motions of a saw.

A scent that smelled like home, like sweet wildflowers and fresh summer grass, crossed his nose and grew stronger. He only recognized her by her picture. She turned into a beautiful full-grown version of the little girl he played with every day since the day she was born, since the day he became a shifter.

"Hey, Squirt." He didn't raise his voice for fear of others hearing him, and he hoped Holly heard him as she passed. Her sharp intake hit his ears, and she turned around. Wide green eyes locked onto him, hurting him in a way he didn't think possible.

"Zachary?" She whispered his name and her eyes filled with moisture. Holly plastered a seductive smirk on her lips and turned toward him. One step and Zachary flinched. She halted. She wasn't the same Holly he used to know. All the wildflowers and summer grass were drowned out by a distinct wild scent of an owl. Holly's seductive look wavered, but she recovered.

"Wolf." The look on her face was inviting, but her snub wasn't.

"Owl." He wasn't as shocked to meet another shifter as she seemed to be.

"What the hell are you doing here?" Accusation leached from her lips that barely moved with her whisper. She didn't have to speak up for him to hear her and vice versa.

"Looking for you."

"You're not..." She swallowed before she tried again. "You're not here for the events?"

"No, I'm not."

Holly's chin quivered.

"Don't cry, Squirt. We need to get you out of here before you can cry."

"You can't. There's no way out, Zachary." Harshness

edged each word. Holly was desolate and her eyes were shells of the little sister he missed having around and last saw so many years ago.

Another girl, similar features and size to Holly's still petite frame, sidled up next to her. Zachary's eyes blinked rapidly and an involuntary growl reverberated through his body. It was a damn good thing he was already sitting or the dizziness and headache would have put him on his ass. She had a scent full of sweet cherries and he wanted to devour her.

Hell of a place to discover his mate.

His focus blurred, but he heard Holly, her words thick like spoken over a swollen tongue muffled in his ears.

"Are you okay?"

"I'm sure he's fine. There's more that would like to place bets." Her melodic inflection cut through the haze, trying to urge Holly to move on.

"Don't leave." His growl tore at his throat.

"What is it, Zachary?" Holly reached for him, but pulled her hand back.

"You know him? Wait. Zachary. That Zachary?"

"Yeah."

Zachary focused his eyes on his mate and as soon as he did, his gut sank to the floor. Her hands didn't hold a tablet like the rest. They were wrapped and ready to fight. Both still stood with practiced seduction and flirtatious expressions, never breaking from their act. No one looking on would think they were having any discussion other than his interest in a fighter.

She was the reverse image of Holly. Her dark hair was pulled tight into two braids exposing the creamy column of her neck. His eyes roamed down her body noting her curves, that he imagined were slimmer than normal, left bare from her outfit.

"What's your name?"

"Fighter names only. Tallon."

Zachary turned his eyes to Holly, demanding with a look she tell him her name.

"Ezaray," she whispered.

"Holly," Ezaray admonished.

"It doesn't matter, Zee. He's leaving." She pinned her eyes on him. Long gone was the little girl. "And he's never coming back here." In her place stood a pint-sized shifter. She marched off for two steps, then corrected the sway of her hips before she sidled up to another group of men.

Ezaray hesitated in front of him.

"Can I touch you?"

"It's not against the rules, but you can't hurt me."

"Never." He waited for her to step closer, then he stood. He caught her leaning into him as he towered over her. His hand lifted and ran down her arm, feeling the muscle beneath her pale skin. With the heat that ignited from his touch, his weakness grew and he had to sit back down.

He was eye level to her wrapped hands. His veins throbbed with the quick rage of rushing blood. All he wanted was to tear the throats out of every man in here.

"You fight well?" Zachary wished he sounded smoother as he saw Ezaray flinch when he spoke.

"Yeah, I do."

"What happens if you lose?"

"Depends how often I lose."

"You going to win tonight?" He tried to instil confidence and encouragement.

"Probably not." Ezaray backed away, her eyes lost in his, before she turned away into the crowd.

Zachary had to watch his mate fight. A fight that could be for her life.

To get your copy and continue reading, go to the link below to buy Silver Chains, Wounded Winds Book Three. http://www.books2read.com/woundedwinds3

ABOUT THE AUTHOR

Looking at a crossroads, Sarah chose to write. With a deep love of anything romance, it was natural that romance stories flowed into her journal. From the East Coast and living in Alberta, Canada, she enjoys life with her family and the beauty of the province around her. She gets hilariously excited when new stories and characters pop in her head and can't wait to write them out whether in the sub-genres of romantic suspense or paranormal romance. She hopes her readers enjoy her stories as much as she enjoys writing them.

You can find Sarah on Facebook and Instagram @author-sarahu, in her reader group Sarah's Wild Ones, and on BookBub

9 781777 301156